<u>What Kids Say About Carole Marsh Mysteries . . .</u>

I love the real locations! Reading the book always makes me want to go and visit them all on our next family vacation. My Mom says maybe, but I can't wait!

One day, I want to be a real kid in one of Ms. Marsh's mystery books. I think it would be fun, and I think I am a real character anyway. I filled out the application and sent it in and am keeping my fingers crossed!

History was not my favorite subject till I started reading Carole Marsh Mysteries. Ms. Marsh really brings history to life. Also, she leaves room for the scary and fun.

I think Christina is so smart and brave. She is lucky to be in the mystery books because she gets to go to a lot of places. I always wonder just how much of the book is true and what is made up. Trying to figure that out is fun!

Grant is cool and funny! He makes me laugh a lot!!

I like that there are boys and girls in the story of different ages. Some mysteries I outgrow, but I can always find a favorite character to identify with in these books.

They are scary, but not too scary. They are funny. I learn a lot.
There is always food which makes me hungry. I feel like I am there.

What Adults Say About Carole Marsh Mysteries . . .

I think kids love these books because they have such a wealth of detail.
I know I learn a lot reading them! It's an engaging way to look at the
history of any place or event. I always say I'm only going to read one
chapter to the kids, but that never happens—it's always two or three, at
least!   —Librarian

Reading the mystery and going on the field trip—Scavenger Hunt in
hand—was the most fun our class ever had! It really brought the place
and its history to life. They loved the real kids characters and all the
humor. I loved seeing them learn that reading is an experience to
enjoy!   —4th grade teacher

Carole Marsh is really on to something with these unique mysteries.
They are so clever; kids want to read them all. The Teacher's Guides
are chock full of activities, recipes, and additional fascinating
information. My kids thought I was an expert on the subject—and
with this tool, I felt like it! —3rd grade teacher

My students loved writing their own Real Kids/Real Places mystery
book! Ms. Marsh's reproducible guidelines are a real jewel. They
learned about copyright and more & ended up with their own book
they were so proud of! —Reading/Writing Teacher

The Ghost of the

GRAND CANYON

CAROLE MARSH
MYSTERIES™

by

Carole Marsh

Copyright © 2004 by Carole Marsh

Published by Gallopade International/Carole Marsh Books. Printed in the United States of America.

Editorial Assistant: Carrie Runnals

Cover design: Vicki DeJoy; Editor: Jenny Corsey; Graphic Design: Steve St. Laurent; Layout and footer design: Lynette Rowe; Photography: Michael Boylan.

Also available:
The Ghost of the Grand Canyon Teacher's Guide

Gallopade is proud to be a member of these educational organizations and associations:

International Reading Association
National Association for Gifted Children
The National School Supply and Equipment Association
Association for Supervision and Curriculum Development
The National Council for the Social Studies
Museum Store Association
Association of Partners for Public Lands

NSSEA

ASCD

This book is dedicated to Lulu, Chief, Grampy, Grammy, Mee Maw and Paw Paw—three sets of beloved grandparents to the real Dani and Marisa Runnals.

This book is a complete work of fiction. All events are fictionalized, and although the first names of real children are used, their characterization in this book is fiction.

For additional information on Carole Marsh Mysteries, visit: www.carolemarshmysteries.com

Message from the rim

20 YEARS AGO . . .

As a mother and an author, one of the fondest periods of my life was when I decided to write mystery books for children. At this time (1979) kids were pretty much glued to the TV, something parents and teachers complained about the way they do about video games today.

I decided to set each mystery in a real place—a place kids could go and visit for themselves after reading the book. And I also used real children as characters. Usually a couple of my own children served as characters, and I had no trouble recruiting kids from the book's location to also be characters.

Also, I wanted all the kids—boys and girls of all ages—to participate in solving the mystery. And, I wanted kids to learn something as they read. Something about the history of the location. And I wanted the stories to be funny.

That formula of real+scary+smart+fun served me well. The kids and I had a great time visiting each site and many of the events in the stories actually came out of our experiences there. (For example, we really did visit the El Tovar, ride mules down into the Grand Canyon and fly back out in a helicopter!)

I love getting letters from teachers and parents who say they read the book with their class or child, then visited the historic site and saw all the places in the mystery for themselves. What's so great about that? What's great is that you and your children have an experience that bonds you together forever. Something you shared. Something you both cared about at the time. Something that crossed all age levels—a good story, a good scare, a good laugh!

20 years later,

Carole Marsh

Christina Yother **Grant Yother** **Danielle Runnals** **Marisa Runnals**

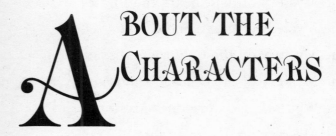

ABOUT THE CHARACTERS

Christina Yother, 9, from Peachtree City, Georgia

Grant Yother, 7, from Peachtree City, Georgia
Christina's brother

Danielle Runnals, 10, as Marisa, from Peachtree City, Georgia

Marisa Runnals, 8, as Dani, from Peachtree City, Georgia

The many places featured in the book actually exist and are worth a visit! Perhaps you could read the book and follow the trail these kids went on during their mysterious adventure!

Titles in the Carole Marsh Mysteries Series

Books and Teacher's Guides are available at booksellers, libraries, school supply stores, museums, and many other locations!

CONTENTS

1 Bound for Adventure

"We're almost in Arizona," Grant said, peering out the airplane window. His bouncing knee bumped the tray table causing little lemon-lime soda drops to leap onto Christina's new hot pink cargo pants. She didn't notice. She was too distracted by the Grand Canyon Suite orchestra music blaring from her CD player headset and too busy scanning the horizon for mountains to appear through the haze.

Finally, Christina felt the dampness on her leg. She yanked the headset from her ears. "Grant!" she exclaimed, pulling her eyes from the window and gaping at her soda-dotted pants. "Stop! Watch what you're doing!"

Grant's eyes dropped from the window to Christina's pants. "Uh, oh," he said with a gulp.

"You're ruining my new pants Mimi gave me," Christina

whined. "I'm going to be all sticky when this stuff dries...Yuck!"

"I'm sorry!" Grant apologized. "I'm just so excited to see the Grand Canyon, my knee can't keep still. Look, even when I try to hold it down, it just keeps hopping."

Christina swabbed her pants with a napkin, resisting the temptation to, once again, play with the cool zippers on the pockets. The sides of her mouth turned slowly upwards as she noticed Grant's futile attempts to stop his kangaroo-on-coffee knee. He finally gave up and looked helplessly at Christina. They both exploded into laughter.

Suddenly, a loud voice boomed over their heads.

"This is your captain speaking," the man said.

"Hey," Grant said. "It's Captain Speaking. That's the same guy that flew our plane to Alaska."

"Grant," Christina said, trying hard not to laugh at her little brother. "This is the captain speaking, as in...*talking*. That's not his name." Sometimes, Christina thought, experienced nine-year-old big sisters had to cut their younger brothers some slack. After all, it wasn't so long ago that she was seven and not as smart as she was now.

"Ohhhhh," Grant said. Then, in a smaller voice, "Oh." His face reddened as he sneaked glances from side to side to see if anyone else had heard his silly comment.

The pilot's words grabbed their attention. *"We will be touching down in Flagstaff in just a few moments,"* the captain continued. *"The weather is a balmy 110 degrees, but don't worry, with only 10 percent humidity, it's quite pleasant."*

"Pleasant?" Christina said, shooting Grant a disbelieving look. They'd been in hot weather before in their hometown of Peachtree City, Georgia, but 100 degrees was the hottest. Christina remembered it exactly, because that was the day Mimi and Papa filled water balloons and put them in the freezer, just until they got slushy, not frozen solid. Then, they took them outside and the whole family, even Mimi, had a water balloon fight. Christina smiled at the memory. Now, that was a good day, she thought, especially eating the huge bowls of ice cream on the back porch afterwards. Her smile faded as she thought of what 110 degrees felt like—a blasting furnace, she imagined.

"It's 5:22 p.m. Navajo time," the pilot continued. Christina's confusion made deep creases between her brows. Before Mimi had a chance to explain, the pilot's voice returned, *"By the way, Navajo time means one hour be-FORE Arizona time."* He added, *"The Navajo Nation observes daylight savings time, but the rest of the state,*

including the Hopi Reservation, which is actually surrounded by the Navajo Nation, does not."

Oh, great, Christina thought. She had a hard enough time keeping her Carole Marsh Mysteries watch set to the right time going from state to state. This was going to be a nightmare. Suddenly, the excitement for her trip to the Grand Canyon was starting to sound not as wonderful as she'd imagined. She usually loved teaming up with Mimi on her adventure trips, but this one was starting to sound a bit more challenging, not to mention sweatier, than any they'd been on before. Mimi always invited Grant and Christina to come along with her on her research trips to get background information for the mystery books she wrote. It seemed every time Grant and Christina accompanied their grandmother, something unexpected happened.

"Mimi?" Grant asked, his voice timid. "What's a Nah-vah-ho?"

"They are the Indians who have lived in the area near the Grand Canyon since the 1400s," Mimi explained.

"Is the lady we're staying with a Navajo Indian?" Christina asked.

"No, actually, she's a Hopi Indian," Mimi reported. "The Hopi have been in Arizona even longer, since the

1100s, believe it or not."

"Wow, that's three hundred years longer than the Navajo and..." Christina was trying to hide her fingers as she counted how many years ago 1100 was from now. She gave up. "That's a really, *really* long time ago," she said to her grandmother.

"About 900 years," Grant said. Christina sighed. Her brother was really good at math.

"I'm looking forward to staying on a real Indian reservation with Nampeyo and her two girls," said Mimi.

"Nam-pay-oh," Grant said, as if saying it more slowly and sounding out each syllable would help him understand its meaning.

"You can call her Nammie," Mimi added. "Evidently, she was named after a famous Indian woman potter and it just so happens she ended up being quite a notable potter, herself."

"I thought you said she was a park ranger, Mimi?" Christina asked.

"Oh, she is," Mimi said. "But she's also become quite well known for her pottery skills."

Grant's nose scooted up his face as though he just ate a whole plate of spinach. He hadn't heard a word after *girl*.

"Wait just a minute," he demanded. "Did you say two

girls? TWO *GIRLS*?"

Mimi nodded, "Grant, you'll be fine. Papa's here for male moral support."

"Yeah, but he *likes* girls," Grant said, his shoulders dropping.

"Two girls? That rocks!" Christina beamed. Mimi shot her one of her famous "watch it" looks, then leaned across the aisle and put her hand on Grant's shoulder.

"Listen, buddy, the younger sister is your age. I'm sure you can find something in common," Mimi said.

"Yeah, Grant, we'll *stick* together," Christina reassured him, pointing at her pants with a smile. Grant looked down at the sticky stains and burst out laughing.

The bell sounded indicating it was okay to unbuckle their seatbelts, so Grant and Christina scurried to gather their belongings.

"Yes, kids, we're sure to have fun," Papa said, with a yawn, rousing from his flight-long nap across the aisle. "And who knows what mystery the Valentine State has in store?"

"Valentine State?" Christina repeated his words in a question.

"Yep," Papa said. "Arizona officially became a state on Valentine's Day in 1912. It was the last of the continental

states to be given a name, so it's also nicknamed the Baby State," Papa said, smiling at Mimi's impressed expression.

"Hey, I know what it's like to be the baby of the group," said Grant. "I like Arizona much better, definitely."

Christina's mind was still stuck on Papa's mystery comment. She wondered what could possibly be in store for them in a place with thousands of years of Native American history. There was bound to be adventure right around the corner.

2 AIRPORT ANXIETY

Papa gallantly struggled to tote Mimi's heavy, new red carryons through the gateway, one bag slung over his shoulder, the other pulled behind him on wobbly black wheels. Christina wondered what Mimi could possibly have packed to make her bags so unwieldy. Whatever it was, Christina bet her allowance it was red. Mimi loved red. Good thing it looked so good on her. Christina liked having a with-it grandmother who was fun. The trick was keeping up with her.

Grant and Christina jumped off the escalator and raced each other to catch up with Mimi and Papa in the baggage claim area to search for their luggage. Grant stood just outside the opening where the bags glided down the conveyer belt, so he'd be the first to see and pull off their suitcases. He was the first to see them, all right, but the

pulling off was the hard part. Papa had to rescue Grant's valiant efforts and keep him from being dragged through baggage claim on a runaway suitcase.

"Papa, I almost had it," Grant whined between breaths. "What's in that thing, anyway? It weighs a ton."

"You'd be surprised at the amount of luggage you need for a trip to the Grand Canyon," Mimi interjected. "We need all kinds of extra gear for hiking and excursion trips."

Before Grant could sound that word out, Christina asked, "What's excursion mean?"

"Fun. It means, fun—and that's all you need to know, just now," Papa said, looking at Mimi and matching her grin.

"Hey, that means it's going to be a surprise!" Christina gleaned, jumping up and down clapping her hands.

As Christina pestered her grandparents to reveal their surprise, her eyes focused on a tall man with long black hair, pulled back in a low-slung ponytail. His shoulders were wide, like one of those professional football players Papa watched on television. The big man turned, revealing a chiseled face with high cheekbones and a strong, jutting jaw. Dark sunglasses hid his eyes, but Christina knew already they'd be piercing. Was he looking at her? He walked in her direction with a confident stride.

Utah

CO

N e w M e x i c o

Arizona

Nevada

CA

Colorado River

Grand Canyon
National Park

North
Rim

South Rim
& Grand
Canyon Village

Colorado River

Colorado River

Lowell
Observatory Flagstaff

GRAND CANYON STATE

Before Christina found words to warn her, the dark man walked right up to Mimi and abruptly tapped her on the shoulder. Mimi spun around.

"Mrs. Marsh?" the man asked, in a voice as deep as the tone of his skin.

"Yes?" Mimi answered his question with one of her own.

"I'm Gusta," he said extending his hand in welcome. "I'm Nampeyo's apprentice."

"Oh, yes," Mimi recovered. "Sorry for the shock. I just assumed we'd take a shuttle to the reservation. I wasn't expecting anyone to know me here."

"Well, I sneaked a peek at your picture in one of the girls' mystery books," Gusta admitted. "They've got your whole mystery series." He took off his dark glasses to reveal eyes much softer than Christina expected. She let out the breath she didn't realize she was holding.

Mimi smiled at the compliment. "I knew I'd like those girls," she said.

"What are their names?" Christina asked, unable to contain her excitement. "How old are they?"

"Nampeyo's daughters are Marisa, nine, and Danielle, seven," Gusta reported, smiling at Christina's enthusiasm.

She looked around and asked, "Where are they?"

Before Gusta had a chance to answer, Grant interjected,

"Are you a park ranger apprentice or a pottery apprentice?" Then he added, "Apprentice means she's training you, right?"

Gusta's attention went from Grant to Christina, not sure which to answer first.

"Kids, give the man a chance here," Mimi said, trying to control her excited grandchildren.

"Oh, that's okay," Gusta said. "Let's see. First, I'm a pottery apprentice. I help Nampeyo glaze and fire the pots. I learn a lot just by watching her. Secondly..." Gusta stole a glance at his watch. "Well, let's see...it's just after 5:45 p.m. The girls are both just finishing up their lessons."

"Lessons?" Christina asked. "They still go to school in July? That's horrible."

"No, no," Gusta smiled. "They are both dancing in next month's traditional Hopi ceremony. Nampeyo will be displaying her pottery in the exhibition."

Christina's eyebrows went up as she focused on her sneakers. She hoped they could go.

Gusta thought for a moment, then said, "Just so you know, they both begged their Mom to skip lessons today, but she wouldn't let them. Nampeyo's pretty strict when it comes to teaching the girls about their heritage. They'll appreciate it in the long run, but they were pretty

disappointed." His smile warmed his whole face. Christina looked into his warm brown eyes and smiled too. She liked the way Gusta's accent made his words sound.

"By the time we get back," Gusta continued, "they'll be chomping at the bit to meet you." Christina's smile widened in anticipation.

"Oh, great," Grant said, without enthusiasm. "Three against one. It just doesn't seem fair."

"Grant," Mimi gently scolded.

Gusta let out a small laugh. "Don't worry, kiddo. Wait until you meet Danielle. She's not your average girl. She goes strictly by Dani and is the fastest kid in her class, not to mention the reservation." Grant's eyebrows climbed up his forehead and his frown started turning upside down.

Gusta added, "Dani's not afraid to get dirty either, and she climbs trees with the best of them." Grant relaxed and actually looked like he might want to meet the girls. Well, at least one of them.

Everyone grabbed a bag and followed Gusta to the parking lot. They walked from the airport exit directly into an attached parking garage and helped Gusta find his black van protected in a dark shaded spot. Christina and Grant piled into the van's back seat among the luggage that didn't fit in the cargo area. At least there was enough

room to buckle up.

"Man, there sure are a lot of strange names in Arizona," Grant said.

"Shhhh, Grant," Christina said, looking up front to see if Gusta had heard him. He was too busy listening to Mimi talk about the flight. "Just because their names are different, doesn't mean they're strange."

"I didn't say they were," Grant defended himself.

"Anyway, I like their names," Christina said. "I can't wait to meet Nampeyo and especially her two girls." Grant rolled his eyes. "Besides," Christina said, "Danielle and Marisa are not strange names, at all. There are girls at our school with those names."

"Whatever," Grant responded.

As soon as Gusta pulled the van out of the parking garage, sunlight hit the windshield and infiltrated the vehicle with its powerful rays. The kids' faces instantly scrunched up in matching squints.

Gusta looked back at them in the rearview mirror.

"It sure is bright here, isn't it?" he asked. The blinded children nodded. "Just wait until you step outside and feel the heat," Gusta said, covering his smiling eyes with dark shades.

"Hey," Grant whispered so only Christina could hear.

"Didn't Mimi say that Nampeyo's friends called her Nammie?"

"Yes, so?" Christina asked.

"Then why doesn't he?" Grant asked more as a statement than a question.

Hmmm, Christina thought. That's a good question.

3 FUN IN FLAGSTAFF

Christina's eyes finally adjusted to the bright light and she was able to take in the view. It wasn't what she expected. So far all she saw were trees, trees, and more trees, sort of like driving on some of the back roads in Georgia—where was the canyon?

Her mind started wandering. She felt lucky to have been able to visit so many different states with her grandparents. When she made her timeline poster project in school, she was almost embarrassed to see on paper how many places she'd actually been by the time she was in fourth grade. None of her classmates had been to even half as many places.

"Where are we?" Grant asked, breaking Christina's train of thought. She noticed that they were now coming into a town.

"This is Flagstaff," Gusta said. "Legend has it that back in 1876 Thomas McMillan led a group of pilgrims here. He cut a pine tree to use as a staff for the American flag for a Fourth of July celebration and left it standing afterwards. It became the trail marker and later when the post office was built and the town was settled, the settlers agreed to call it Flagstaff."

Christina smiled at that. It sounded so simple.

"I thought pilgrims came to America on the Mayflower and landed at Plymouth Rock?" Grant asked.

"Pilgrims are any travelers to a new place," Mimi explained. "Sort of like us today!"

"How about we take a drive up Mars Hill and take a peak at Flagstaff from the Lowell Observatory," Gusta suggested.

"Mars Hill?" asked Grant. He was intrigued by anything to do with outer space.

"I've heard of that place," Papa said. "Percival Lowell constructed a telescope there in the late 1800s to study the planet Mars, right?"

"That's right," Gusta said. "A lot of folks made fun of him for thinking that water may have sparked life on Mars."

"Wow, wouldn't he have been thrilled to know of the recent explorations on the Red Planet," Mimi said. "Too

bad he didn't live in the 21st century. He'd probably be one of the scientists working with the twin-rovers, *Opportunity* and *Spirit*."

"Yes," Gusta said. "I just read about how they've found bedrock that resembles layered rocks laid down by lakebeds and lava on Earth—that supports Lowell's theories."

"Boy," Grant whispered to Christina. "Gusta sure seems to know a lot of history, science, and current events. He should be a teacher." Christina nodded.

They pulled into the parking lot of the observatory, and Gusta unlocked the doors. As the car doors slowly opened, the heat seeped through the vehicle and swallowed up Christina, making it hard for her to breathe. It reminded her of being in the sauna at her Mom's health club.

As soon as Grant stepped out of the van, he bent over at the waist and quickly unzipped his cargo pants around the knees, letting the lower half of the pants fall around his ankles.

"Instant shorts!" he exclaimed, with a smile from ear to ear. "Give it a try, Christina," he suggested.

Christina crawled out of the van, turned her nose up at her brother's fashion flaw, and swiped the fast-forming

sweat from her forehead. "No way," she said. Even though she'd love to have shorts on right now, a girl's got to have some style. Dragging pant legs around her ankles wasn't exactly what she'd call fashionable.

They climbed the steps to the observatory and looked out over the town of Flagstaff. Christina was amazed at the railroads coming in and out of the city.

"It looks like a town of toy trains, like the ones you see at those Christmas stores with the cardboard villages," Grant said.

"Yes, it's pretty impressive," said Gusta. "There is so much more to Flagstaff than trains, though. It's a mecca for art and crafts. Nampeyo displays her pottery at some of the galleries in town. Someday, I hope to do the same."

Christina's attention was drawn to the mountain range. "What are those mountains called?" she asked.

"Those are the sacred San Francisco Peaks, the highest mountains in Arizona," Gusta said.

"Sacred?" Christina asked.

"Yes, the Hopi, Navajo and many other Native Americans believe that the mountains hold spiritual meaning," Gusta said. "Listen, I thought maybe we could stop at the Wupatki National Museum on the way home. It's got stunning architectural stonework from

the ancient Puebloans."

Christina knew it was coming..."Pweb-what?" Grant questioned.

"Pueblos are a type of house built out of sandstone and mud. The Wupatki Pueblo is a four-story dwelling with more than 100 rooms built back in the 1200s."

"Wow! *Everything* is so old here," Grant said.

Before Gusta could respond, his cell phone rang.

"Hello?" Gusta said. Christina could hear a high-pitched voice seeping out around his ear. "Yes, I've got them right here," he said into the mouthpiece. A slow smile formed on his face as he listened to the obviously excited voice on the other end. "Oh, okay," he finally said. "We were going to try to hit the museum, but you're right...okay, we'll meet you there." Gusta hung up the phone and started laughing.

"Evidently, I'm torturing Dani. She can't wait to meet you," he said. "The girls are home, and Nampeyo wants us to meet them for dinner at the El Tovar Hotel."

"A hotel for dinner?" Grant asked.

"Yes, it's a famous hotel built right on the rim of the Grand Canyon. It'll be a great place for you to get your first glimpse of the canyon, not to mention get some of the best food around."

"Sounds great to me," said Papa, rubbing his stomach. "That airplane food is wearing pretty thin."

As Gusta got out of town on the open road, his foot grew heavier and heavier on the gas pedal. Christina started wriggling in her seat until Mimi came to the rescue.

"What's up, Gusta," Mimi joked. "Got too much sedimentary rock in your boots?"

"Oops," Gusta said. "Guess I was focused on getting these kids together. I'll slow down."

"Are those really clean rocks?" Grant asked.

"He thinks you mean *sanitary* rocks," Christina explained.

"Sed-i-men-tary," Gusta corrected gently. "The Grand Canyon is made up of all different kinds of rock pieces that are spread around by wind and water—sedimentary rock."

Christina stared out the window. Where were the rocks? Where was that mother-of-all-holes-in-the-ground— The Grand Canyon? And what secret were Mimi and Papa hiding?

Can't wait for the canyon!

4 HOPI ART HISTORY

The van passed a sign on the side of the road and Gusta read it out loud.

"The Cameron Trading Post," he said pulling the van into a dusty parking lot. "Let's swing in here for a minute. We're ahead of the girls, anyway, and you can sneak a peek at the Little Colorado River."

"The Little Colorado River?" Grant asked. "Where's the big one?"

"Well, the Little Colorado River runs north from here where it meets up with the Colorado River," Gusta said. "The little one is brownish and warm. The big one looks clear and green—very tempting to swim in until you stick your toes in. It's freezing!"

Swimming in cool water sounded like a great idea to Christina after being on a plane for hours and walking

around dripping with sweat.

Stepping out of the van seemed like stepping back in time as they walked on the dirt path among wooden and stone buildings. Just beyond the trading post, Christina could see a rickety old bridge stretched across a gorge.

They pushed open the heavy, wooden doors of the trading post and heard the eerie screech of old floorboards as they made their way through rows of dry and canned goods.

Christina never saw anything like a trading post in Peachtree City. She looked up to see countless pairs of pants and shirts hanging from the rafters, below rows and rows of cheap souvenirs, candy, and munchies. This place was like a convenience store, department store, and museum all rolled into one. Christina felt the money Mimi had given her for the trip burning a hole in her zippered pocket.

Mimi read her mind. "Now don't start itching to spend all your cash in one place," she said. "Gusta, you better show us that river soon or this could get ugly."

"Oh, Mimi," Grant whined. "Can't we just buy one thing?"

"We'll see," she said. "Let's go get our picture on the bridge over the gorge, okay?"

Christina's feet froze at the thought of standing on that wobbly thing, but with an encouraging nudge from Mimi, she moved past souvenirs to what appeared to be an art gallery filled with authentic Native American pottery, carvings, jewelry, and beautiful baskets. Colorful woven rugs hung on the walls on either side of the fireplace.

"Hey, take a look over here real quick," Gusta suggested. "This is some of Nampeyo's pottery." He pointed to three stunning, painted pots.

"They're incredible..." Mimi said wistfully, admiring the subtle colors glazed into the clay pots. "I had no idea my park ranger pal did such amazing work."

"The women in her family have passed down their top secret technique from generation to generation, and now she's teaching her girls," Gusta said. He looked at the kids. "I bet you'll get a chance to get your hands dirty too, once we get to the reservation."

"Wow, that'd be great," Christina said, trailing her fingers over the smoothness of a striking black and white pot.

"Nampeyo has made quite a name for herself," Gusta said. "In fact, she's considered one of the best Hopi potters around—her work is admired by art connoisseurs and envied by other not-so-talented potters." A concerned

look skipped across his face, but was quickly veiled with a smile as he noticed Grant's confused expression.

"A connoisseur is an expert," Gusta informed him. "They're people who judge how good your art is—like in a contest."

Grant gave him a grateful grin. He inspected the printed woven rugs on the wall. "Those rugs look like story books with all the different animals and lizards on them."

Christina wasn't paying attention. She was still thinking about what Gusta had said about the jealous potters. It reminded her of the time in art class when Nikki's picture of jungle animals turned out much better than hers. At the time, she wanted to rip up Nikki's picture in frustration. It wasn't fair. Christina had worked so hard, but there was no mistaking that Nikki's picture was the best in the class. Everyone, including Mrs. Olander, gushed over how great it was. Christina remembered how Mimi told her the easiest way to make herself unhappy was to compare herself to others. She encouraged Christina to focus on doing her own personal best. She was reminded of how good it felt, the next time she visited Mimi and Papa, to find her jungle picture hanging on their refrigerator.

Mimi was mesmerized by Nampeyo's pottery. Papa sneaked a peek at the price tag and quickly grabbed Mimi's

elbow to lead her toward the door. "We need to get this lady out of here, before she spends all our green," he said to Gusta with a playful grin.

"I can't help it if I appreciate fine art," Mimi said in a bit of a huff. She pulled her arm from Papa's grasp.

"Oh, I'm sure Nampeyo can cut you a good deal on one of the pots she has back at the shop," Gusta assured her.

As they headed toward the back door, Papa glanced over his shoulder to see Grant eyeing some decorated wooden figurines.

"Those are unique, aren't they, Grant?" Gusta asked, coming up behind him. Grant nodded without moving his eyes from the colorful feathered headdress of the largest one.

"These are called kachina dolls," Gusto said. "They are made by the Hopi Indians who call them *Tihu*."

"Dolls?" Grant said, stepping back and pulling his hands away from the figures.

"Don't worry, they aren't just for girls," Gusta assured him. "People have been collecting them since the mid-1800s, and their origin dates back way before then."

"Ohhhh, those are so cool," Christina piped up. "Do they have any particular meaning?"

"Well, actually, they do have important meaning

because they are symbols of kachina or katsina spirits."

"Spirits?" Grant said with a startled expression. "Do you mean like ghosts?"

"Well, sort of," Gusta said. "According to Hopi beliefs, kachinas are kind spirit beings who live among the Hopi and have power to exercise control over natural forces. They believe that kachinas help the Hopi in many of their everyday activities, including punishing those who offend them."

"Yikes!" Grant said with wide eyes. "I better remember not to upset Dani or Marisa, huh?"

"That might be a good idea, Grant," Gusta said, with a mischievous laugh.

They walked through the back door, down the porch steps, and onto a bridge swinging by ropes across the gorge. Christina took tentative steps onto the bridge of wooden slats. She could peer through the cracks down to the water and rocks far below. The bridge swayed with each step they took. It reminded Christina of being suspended in space in one of those carnival Ferris wheel rides. Even Papa's comforting hand in hers didn't do much to shoo away the butterflies that gathered in her tummy.

Christina wasn't so sure seeing the narrow brown river far below was worth the risk, but she agreed to stay on it

long enough for Gusta to snap a picture of them with Grant's new digital camera.

Later, as they sat in the backseat on the drive to the hotel, Grant pushed the 'review' button on his camera. The way he gasped made Christina pull off her headphones and ask what the matter was.

"Look!" Grant said, holding the camera toward her with a trembling hand. Christina looked at the picture glowing from the camera screen.

"Yuck, look at my hair," she said. She thought for a moment. "The wind wasn't even blowing. Why was my hair standing on end like that?"

"Christina, who cares about your hair—LOOK!" Grant said again, this time pointing at a cloudy area on the picture behind their heads. Her face stiffened. Her eyes widened as the figure of a phantom warrior clad in a red feather headdress became clearer. It looked like the kachina doll Grant had been looking at just before they walked out on the bridge. But was he a real person? Dangerous? Or was he a spirit? And why was he watching them?

5 ENCOUNTER AT EL TOVAR

As they drove towards the El Tovar hotel, Gusta continued to fill them in on facts about the Grand Canyon and local Indian traditions. Christina could tell from the changing colors in the sky that the sun was slowly headed toward the West where it would soon sleep for the night. It was getting dark out! She wished, now, Gusta would get a bit more of that sedimentary rock in his shoes. They were going to miss seeing the huge hole in the ground!

"The El Tovar hotel was built in 1905 out of limestone blocks and logs from Oregon," Gusta said.

"That's fascinating," said Mimi. "It's hard to believe that a hotel built on the edge of a canyon could withstand nature for nearly 100 years."

As they pulled into the dusty parking lot of the El Tovar hotel, it seemed to Christina like some kind of bad joke.

The sun was just ducking behind the canyon walls, sending stripes of orange, red, and yellow across canyon sheets of rock. The colors seemed to glow, reminding Christina of the popsicle with the different layers Papa had bought her and Grant at Disney World—except without the neon blue and green. From her vantage point in the back of the van, she immediately noticed that the gigantic stone hotel with its huge front porch *really* was built right on the edge of the canyon.

"Why did they build the canyon so close to the hotel?" Grant asked in a serious tone.

"Ha, ha, very funny," Christina said, in an attempt to cover up for Grant's silly comment as she waited for him to get out of the van.

"Hurry up, Grant," Christina wailed, a bit shriller than she had intended. "The sun is already going down. We're going to miss it!"

"Miss what?" Grant said.

"The canyon!" Christina exclaimed, frustrated with Grant's dilly-dallying. She crawled over his lap to get to the door and struggled to open it, until Gusta pressed the button that unlocked it and released it automatically.

As Christina popped out of the van and ran toward the hotel, it was though a curtain was being pulled across a

theater stage in front of her. She caught a glimpse of the majesty of the canyon walls stretched endlessly in either direction, but before she could even begin to appreciate it, it was gone. The sun dipped below the cliffs and darkness crept into the canyon from both sides, swiftly meeting in the middle in a hazy dusk. The gorgeous colors had been instantly replaced with shades of gray.

"I didn't even get to see the canyon," Christina said to herself. "Well, just for a second," she corrected herself, "but that hardly counts."

"That was absolutely gorgeous," Mimi said, catching up with Christina and trying to catch her breath. She put her arm around Christina's shoulder. Then, sensing Christina's disappointment, she said, "Don't worry. We'll have plenty of chance to see the canyon, Christina. After all, we're going to be here for more than ten days."

Christina shook off her regret and allowed Mimi to lead her over to where Gusta led Papa and Grant up the steps to the hotel veranda. In the dim lighting, the rustic porch furniture appeared as old as the building. They stepped into the main lobby and stood still for a moment allowing their eyes to adjust to the dim lighting of the lodge. Christina liked the log walls in the main foyer, but upon further inspection found something she truly did *not* like.

The soft, sad eyes of a deer, or a deer head, to be more specific, stared her in the face. She couldn't blink. She couldn't speak. She couldn't even swallow the fast-forming lump in her throat. She forced her eyes away from the deer and scanned the walls in horror to see numerous animal heads—deer, antelope, and moose. She even saw a stuffed squirrel with a white tail holding an acorn up to his mouth as though he were about to eat it.

Yuck! Christina's stomach felt queasy. The glass eyes followed her wherever she moved, pleading with her. She quickly asked to go to the restroom. She didn't want to be rude, but she had to get out of there fast. The hostess pointed down a dark narrow hallway to the ladies room.

"We'll be in the dining room," she heard Mimi call after her, oblivious to her uneasiness.

As Christina stared at her feet, trying not to notice any more animal faces in the hallway, she was suddenly grabbed by the elbow and swiftly tugged into an open doorway. Before she could steady herself, she lost her balance and lay face down on a chilly tiled floor. The coolness felt good, until she realized it was a *bathroom* floor.

"Eww, gross!" Christina cried, scrambling to get up.

"Oh, oops!" cried a voice that sounded very much like

her own. "I'm so sorry. I didn't mean to make you fall."

Christina looked up to see a tall blonde-haired, blue-eyed girl wearing a black straw cowboy hat extending her hand.

"I'm Marisa!" she exclaimed. Christina's heart skipped a beat, and an instant smile replaced her worried expression as she accepted Marisa's hand and stood up.

"You are?" Christina said in disbelief. This girl didn't look anything like someone who lived on an Indian reservation. She looked more like the girls from Christina's hometown. She had expected her to have the same Native American characteristics as Gusta—dark hair and dark eyes. The only resemblance this girl had to a Native American was deeply tanned skin and braids.

All at once, a large, rushing sound erupted from behind the stall door and out popped a smaller version of Marisa with bangs and green eyes. She even had the same kind of hat, just shorter braids.

"Hi!" Dani shouted. She held out her hand for Christina to shake but before she could, Marisa smacked Dani's wrist, causing her hand to fall to her side.

"Eww, gross!" Marisa shouted. "Dani, wash your hands first! Yuck!"

Marisa reminded Christina of herself and the way

she always tried to remind Grant to do the right thing. Of course, Grant found it annoying and told her she was bossy.

Dani's cheeks flushed. "Oh, yeah, I forgot," she said with a smirk. She squirted a whole handful of liquid soap from the dispenser into her palm, turned on the water, and started rubbing her hands together. A mountain of bubbles filled the sink as she talked, but she didn't notice, because the whole time her face was turned toward Christina as she chatted nonstop.

"You finally got here," Dani said. "Well, actually, we just got here too, but we've been so excited to meet you. We are going to have so much fun. Did you guys see our Mom out there? She's at a table. You're gonna love this place. The food is great and wait until you see the view!"

"Geez, Dani," Marisa scolded. "Take a breath and let the girl speak."

They both looked at Christina expectantly waiting for her to say something.

"Um," Christina murmured. "Let's go out and find our folks. I'd like to meet your Mom."

"Don't you have to go to the bathroom?" asked Dani.

"Actually, no," Christina said. "I just had to get away from all those animal heads out there."

"Aren't they gross?" Marisa agreed. "They give me the creeps."

"Oh, what a bunch of sissies," Dani said.

"Where's your brother, Grant?" she asked in a quest to find someone a bit less thin-skinned.

They found him sitting in the lobby staring up in awe at all the animals.

"Wow! This is so cool!" he said when he saw them coming down the hallway. "Hey, Christina, look at the size of that moose's antlers!"

"No, thank you," Christina said, shielding her eyes and heading for the dining room, hoping there weren't animal heads hanging where she had to eat.

Marisa introduced herself quickly to Grant and hurried to follow Christina, but Dani plunked right down in the chair next to Grant's and said, "Hi, I'm Dani." Without waiting for him to introduce himself, she added, "Wouldn't it be cool to be out in the wilderness and come face to face with a wild moose?"

Grant turned his face towards hers, and they instinctually shared the same vision of being in the forest just waiting for their shot—their photo shot!

"That camera you've got there would be perfect," Dani said.

"Yep," Grant said, fingering the digital camera strap around his neck, reconsidering his previous opinion that all girls were wimps.

Grant brought the camera up to his face, and zoomed in close enough to block out the surrounding walls until all he could see through the viewfinder was moose face and antlers.

"Now, this picture will look like I came across a live moose in the woods," he said.

"Trick photography," Dani said. "The next best thing to being there!"

As they headed for their table, neither of the kids noticed the face at the window watching them.

6 GOOD FOOD— GREAT FRIENDS

By the time the kids made it into the dining room, the adults were seated at the table chatting with a pretty lady that Christina correctly assumed was Nampeyo.

"Hey kids," Mimi said, waving them over. "Come meet my friend, Nammie." Grant and Dani caught up with Christina and Marisa just before they reached the table.

Grant and Christina shook hands with Nammie, looked her in the eye, smiled, and said 'hello'–just the way their Dad had taught them. He always stressed that they must be polite to adults, other kids too, but especially adults.

It took Christina a moment to speak. She couldn't get over how much Nammie resembled photos of the Native Americans she'd seen in her history book. She had high

cheekbones and a strong jaw. Her long black hair was pulled back in a thick braid, and she wore lots of turquoise jewelry and a straw cowboy hat just like her daughters.

"Hey, how come you guys look so different from your Mom?" Grant blurted. Christina cringed, but Marisa, Dani, Gusta and Nammie just broke out laughing.

"You've got to love a guy who's not afraid to speak up," Nammie said with a smile. She put her hand on Grant's head and gave it a tender squeeze. "Grant, Dani and Marisa are my children, just like you and Christina are your parents' children. They are sisters, and I adopted them when they were babies. We may look different on the outside, but inside, we are a loving family through and through just like yours."

"Oh okay," Grant said, satisfied with her explanation.

Just then, a waitress came to the table to take their order.

"What will you have, kids?" Mimi asked.

"If you don't mind," Nammie said. "I'd love to order for you, so you get a good taste of all the traditional foods."

"Guess that means no chicken nuggets," Grant whispered to Christina, who was busy looking wistfully at the window. She wasn't paying attention. She was too busy thinking about the view. If it were daytime, she

thought, they'd be able to see forever from this spot. Now all she could see was her own reflection mirrored by the darkness outside.

"Oh, don't worry," reassured Nammie, as though Christina had shared her thoughts out loud. "It'll be there when you get up tomorrow. You and the girls can hike down the canyon and have a picnic lunch."

"All by ourselves?" Grant asked, a bit excited, a bit nervous.

"Oh, yeah," said Dani. "We do it all the time." She looked at him with an unspoken challenge, and then voiced it. "You aren't afraid, are you?"

"No way," Grant said. "I LAUGH in the face of danger."

While the others were talking, Christina noticed something out of the corner of her eye. She glanced back at her reflection to see a tall man standing behind her dressed in an Indian headdress. What? When she turned around, all she saw was the bald head of another visitor sitting behind her. She looked back at the window and saw only her own reflection. I must be seeing things—delirious with exhaustion, she thought.

Suddenly, the waitress showed up with heaping plates of authentic southwestern cuisine. The plates were piled high with mounds of blue and yellow cornmeal, mild red

and green chilies, dark brown blobs of beans with snowy sour cream, shredded lettuce, and a neon-green avocado whip called guacamole. Salty fried tortilla chips stuck out of the top like banners and bowls of brightly colored salsa, made with red tomatoes, green chilies, white onion, and cilantro, were laid on the table for chip dipping. Nammie had also ordered some plates of *carne seca*, sun-dried beef simmered with onions and peppers. Grant and Christina were pretty open to trying all the new and different foods, but their favorite were the sopapillas, puffy fried dough served with honey. *Yum!* Christina thought. She wished she could eat sopapillas with every meal.

During the meal, the adults enjoyed catching each other up on the goings-on of their busy lives and the kids got to know each other as they shared stories about their schools, friends, and things they liked to do. Dani and Marisa were fascinated by the adventures Grant and Christina had taken all over the country. The idea of being characters in a mystery book was fun for them to imagine, though Christina didn't always find it so appealing. She liked getting the attention, and sometimes kids even asked her for her autograph, but it could get pretty embarrassing when Mimi put details in her books that Christina preferred nobody knew. She thought Marisa and Dani were

the ones with the interesting lives, living on an Indian reservation, with horses and a mom who was a park ranger and award-winning potter. Their lives seemed so different, but just as interesting.

When their bellies were full and their tongues were tired from talking, it was time to get ready to go to Nammie's house. Christina wished it was still light outside, so she could see the sights driving into the reservation, but she supposed she'd have a chance to see the canyon tomorrow.

She pushed her chair out and stood up. When she stepped back, she heard a crunch under her foot. She lifted her foot and there on the floor laid a stiff red feather with a smashed quill. Shaking, Christina slowly bent down to pick it up and pricked her finger on the tip of the quill.

"Ouch!" Christina cried. A lone drop of blood seeped from her finger onto the plume, disappearing into its crimson.

Hey, what's this?

7 UNIDENTIFIED DRIVING OBJECT

After dinner, all the kids piled in the van with Gusta and Mimi and Papa rode with Nammie. That way, the kids could all be together. Christina thought Gusta sure was a good sport having all these kids in his van, and he didn't even have kids of his own. Or maybe he did.

"Gusta," Christina asked, momentarily missing her own parents, "Are you a Dad?"

Gusta smiled. "No, Christina," he said. "I'm not even married yet. I'm still in art school."

"Do you know any ghost stories?" Christina asked trying not to seem obvious as she fingered the feather through the pocket on her dirty cargo pants.

"*Ghost* stories?" Gusta asked. The kids cheered in unison.

"Tell them about the lady who haunts the cliffs

searching for her husband and sons who were lost on a rafting trip," Dani shouted.

"No. How about the story of one-armed John Wesley Powell?" Marisa countered from the back seat.

"Oh, Dani," Gusta said. " John Wesley Powell is not a ghost. He was the first man to travel down the Colorado River."

"Did you say one arm?" Grant asked.

"Yea," said Dani. "He lost it fighting in the Civil War and..."

"How do you lose an arm?" Grant interrupted, already worried that it was something that could happen to him.

Christina tugged at her own arm in the dark, hoping no one would notice. Weren't these things permanently attached?

"He probably got shot," Dani said thinking aloud. "And maybe they couldn't fix it, so they had to amputate."

"Eww, gross," Christina said.

"Anyway," Gusta said. "John Wesley Powell was the first man to explore the bottom of the canyon and take a crew of men all the way down the Colorado River."

"Did they make it?" asked Grant.

"Well, some did," Dani said. "Some chickened out and left the boat and ended up getting snatched and murdered

by Indians." She was enjoying the look of suspense on her new friend's faces.

"But not John Wesley," she added. "He made it to the end to a lake."

"Yeah," Marisa began with raised brows, "They say, you can still see the one-armed ghost exploring deep into the canyon in search of his lost men if you camp down there at night."

"That's not true," said Gusta. "You are going to scare these kids to death."

"I'm not scared," Grant said. "But we aren't planning any overnight canyon camping trips are we?"

Christina asked, "Have you...have you ever seen a ghost that looked like a kachina doll?"

"Kachina doll?" Dani asked with a giggle.

"Yeah, with a red headdress," Christina said, trying to sound lighthearted.

"Oh, kachinas," Marisa said, "That's the spirits, not the dolls. Supposedly, they are kind and protect the Hopis, but I've never seen one."

"Oh," Christina let out the air she was holding, but sucked it right back in when Gusta swiftly jerked the steering wheel to avoid hitting a huge black figure speeding down the center of the road.

"Whoa!" they all yelled. Gusta brought the van to a screeching halt just on the edge of a ditch.

"What was that?" Grant yelled.

"Whew! Is everyone alright?" Gusta asked, his forehead wrinkling like an accordion. He parked the van on the side of the road and put the hazard flashers on. He opened the door, stepped outside and looked in the direction the black creature had gone.

"Was that a monster?" Grant asked in a shaky voice. "Was it a UFO?"

"An Unidentified Flying Object?" Marisa asked. "More like a UDO—an Unidentified Driving Object."

"No," Gusta interrupted. "It was some kind of vehicle, maybe a pickup truck, traveling fast, really fast, without lights."

"That is crazy," Marisa said. "Who in the world would even attempt that?"

"Maybe someone trying to get away or trying to hide something," Christina said. "Someone who doesn't want to be seen."

Gusta sat back in the driver's seat, pulled the seat belt and buckled it tight across his chest. Christina could see his hands shaking on the wheel.

"We're okay, everything's okay," Gusta assured them.

Christina thought it sounded like he was also trying to convince himself. "We've only got a few more miles up to the mesa to the reservation. Let's get back and see if the others saw anything suspicious."

The children nervously chatted as they drove up the 7,200-foot Black Mesa. Marisa explained that there were three major mesas surrounded by low altitude deserts and gullies. They lived on the Walpi Mesa along with others who liked the Hopi traditions, but also wanted to have an American lifestyle and work and go to school outside the reservation. Originally, the pueblos were built up high on the mesas for protection from Navajo and Apache Indians. Gusta explained that since the Navajo reservation surrounded the Hopi reservation, some conflict still existed between those who didn't want to give up old traditions.

Their chattering turned into silence as they drove up the dusty drive and noticed blue lights flashing through the sky. When they got closer to the stone and mud-built pueblo, they realize the lights were coming from three police cars parked right outside the door of Nammie's pottery shop.

"What in the world?" Gusta wondered out loud.

"We've been robbed!" Nammie screamed as she came

running out to the van. Gusta stepped out of the van and Nammie grabbed his arms and repeated, "Gusta, we've been robbed—someone took all the pottery we've worked so hard on for the exhibit." Nammie's face was damp with tears. She shook uncontrollably.

The police stayed for hours, and combed the place for clues, but came up empty-handed. Everyone was exhausted, and it was decided that they'd all go to bed and try to figure things out in the morning when they were fresh and their heads had a chance to clear. Christina just couldn't believe they'd been in Arizona less than twenty-four hours and were already knee-deep in a mystery.

That night, all the kids camped out in sleeping bags on Marisa's bedroom floor. Christina marveled at the many dreamcatchers Marisa had hanging on her walls and was reminded of the red feather she found at the restaurant. She pulled it out of her cargo pants pocket and held it tightly under her pillow, not sure why she felt she should keep it a secret. Her mind was reeling, but she was exhausted from the long day and finally fell into a deep sleep.

She dreamed of riding all alone on a raft down a bubbling whitewater river. She tossed in her sleep, just as she tossed in the raft in her dream. She was frightened,

afraid of drowning, but finally she arrived at a calm lake at the end of the river. When she got out of the raft, there on the back, larger than life, sat a kachina in a red headdress. He had guided her raft down the treacherous river to safety. Christina slept peacefully for the rest of the night.

8 READY TO HIT THE TRAILS

The next morning, Christina opened her eyes, rubbed them and rubbed them some more. She couldn't see Marisa. Marisa was missing. She wasn't in her sleeping bag on the floor, and she hadn't crawled up to her bed. Christina even looked under the bed. She woke the others, and they began frantically searching the rest of the pueblo. Finally, the kids decided they should wake the adults. Dani went to the door of her mother's room and pounded frantically.

"Mom," Dani shouted. "Open up! Marisa is missing!"

Mimi and Papa came rushing out of the guest room, tying their robes around their waists.

"What on earth?" Mimi asked.

"Mimi, Marisa is missing!" shouted Christina. In a less stressful moment she may have tried to say that ten times

57

fast, but now was not the time for tongue twisters.

The door to Nammie's room opened and out stepped Marisa. One side of her mouth pulled up to her cheek in embarrassment.

"Hey, guys," she said softly, her chin to her chest. "I'm not missing. I'm right here. I guess I just got a little nervous in the middle of the night and crawled in bed with Mom," she admitted.

"Oh, that's okay," Christina said, not about to make fun of her. After all, she'd been very nervous after what happened, too. "We're just glad we found you."

After breakfast, everyone met in the pottery shop to see if they could find anything that may have been missed in the dark the previous night. Gusta showed up momentarily and helped pick up some of the broken glass from the showcases where Nammie kept her most precious pottery— ancient vessels that had been handed down from generation to generation. Now they were gone.

"Why do you think someone would do such a thing?" Mimi asked. "It's just downright mean, if you ask me."

Gusta and Nammie looked at each other and then back at Mimi.

"Well . . ." Nammie began, then stopped herself.

Christina could tell Nammie had an idea, but didn't want

to say it out loud. She wondered if it had something to do with what Gusta told her yesterday about other potters who were jealous of her work.

Gusta reassured Nammie and she put her thoughts into words. "I really don't want to point fingers, but one theory would lean toward the rivalry that goes back for centuries between the Hopi and Navajo Indians," she said. "Most of us get along, but there are still some folks that hold on to the old ways and refuse to try to live together peacefully. Maybe someone stole the pottery in an attempt to copy it, or sell it, or just keep it for his or her own."

"Nammie, no matter how much you like pottery, you wouldn't keep forty pots for yourself," Gusta said. "Don't kid yourself. Someone stole those pots to sell them on the black market and make a boatload of money, especially the ancient pieces you had locked up in the cabinet."

"Maybe, but what can we do?" Nammie asked, not expecting an answer. "I'm sure the police will conduct an investigation. In the meantime, I've got to get up to the Visitor Center," she said attempting to be lighthearted.

"Nammie," Gusta said. "I'm sure your boss won't mind if you take the day off."

"No, I want to go," she said. "And besides, Mimi and the crew can come along, and I can fill everyone in on some

canyon facts. Maybe by the time we get home this afternoon, the police will come up with something." Nammie tried to be enthusiastic, but Christina could tell that she was still upset.

"And...Christina," said Gusta. "Maybe, you'll finally get a chance to see the Grand Canyon!"

Mimi asked Christina and Grant to follow her to the guest bedroom. She said she had something special to give them before they left. She dug in her huge red suitcase and pulled out two new pairs of hiking boots, one hot pink and the other neon blue.

"Cool," Grant said grabbing the blue pair he assumed were his.

Papa threw them each a backpack stuffed with all kinds of things to use on the trail. The weight of it almost knocked Christina over.

"Gee, Papa," she said. "What's in this thing?"

"Open it and find out," Papa said.

Christina dumped the backpack on the floor while Mimi stood above her braiding her hair to match the style that Nammie, Marisa and Dani wore. Christina picked up each item one by one and put them back into the backpack. There were binoculars, a pink bandanna, bug spray, a water bottle, a flashlight, a Grand Canyon map, a

compass, sunscreen, some snacks, a first-aid kit, clean socks, fresh batteries in a plastic bag, and a few one-dollar bills.

"Everything you'll need for a safe hike," Papa said.

Mimi finished braiding Christina's hair and plopped a straw cowboy hat on top of her head with a tap. "Now, you're ready to go see the canyon," she said.

Christina beamed at her grandmother. "Thanks," she said, as she picked up two hand-held radio-looking things with antennas. As she turned them over in her hand, Grant snatched one.

"Walkie-talkies!" Grant screeched. "How cool! Now, we can talk to each other on the trails!"

"Cool," Christina beamed.

"And look," Grant said. "I've got beef jerky, trail mix, and a magnifying glass." Grant looked through the glass and instantly his eye grew fifty times larger than normal, making him look like some kind of gross prehistoric bug.

9 FIRST CLUE

As the adults finished getting ready, the children ventured outside into the early morning fog to see what they could find. Grant bent over looking through his new magnifying glass at the dusty ground, hunting for footprints.

"Grant," Christina said, "You aren't going to find anything. How are you going to tell whose footprints are in this dust, anyway?"

"You never know," Grant said walking around the side of the pottery shop.

Moments later, a muffled sound erupted from Christina's backpack. It took her a moment to realize it was the sound of Grant's garbled voice coming over the walkie-talkie. She rummaged through the bag, pressed the button, and spoke into the little microphone.

"Grant, what did you say? I couldn't hear you," she said.

"Come back...(his voice cut out)...check (more garble) out," Grant said.

"Grant!" Christina yelled into the walkie-talkie. "You have to push the button down while you are talking or I won't be able to hear you." Marisa and Dani giggled over her shoulder.

"Hey, okay," he said, starting to get the hang of the new-fangled device. "What is this place?" he asked, as he spotted a wooden shack behind the pueblo.

Marisa grabbed the walkie-talkie from Christina and pushed the button while she ran around the house, "Grant, don't go back there!" she said with alarm.

She met up with Grant just as he was jiggling the padlock. "We aren't allowed in there," Marisa said. "That's where the kiln—the oven for firing the pottery—is kept. The heat is what makes the colors so vivid and gives the pots their pretty sheen."

Christina and Dani huffed from their sprint to catch up.

"Yeah," Dani said. "My mom won't let us back here, because she's afraid we'll get burned, so we better go back out front."

Grant's ears were listening, but his eyes were occupied with something else. Beside the shack on a black rock, he

spotted some sort of small white etchings. He took his magnifying glass over to the rock and tried to figure out what it said.

"Grant, what are you doing?" asked Christina.

"Look! I think I found something," Grant said. "Maybe it's some kind of clue. Those marks look like letters, but it's not written in English."

"Whoever wrote that sure didn't have Ms. Coleman for a teacher," Dani said. "If I wrote like that in her class, she'd make me write each word over three times each, until I got it right."

"You know," Marisa said. "Maybe it was written by someone pretty young, or maybe since it was scratched into the rock like that it was difficult to write clearly."

"It almost looks like chalk," Christina said.

"You may be right," Marisa said rubbing one of the letters.

"Wait," Grant squealed. "We need to copy it down before you smear it. It looks like a clue."

"Kids!" They heard Papa bellow from the driveway. "Let's get going. Where are you?"

Marisa quickly scribbled the letters down on her small notepad, shoved it in her backpack, and they all took off for the van.

It's our first clue!

10 DANI THE DECODER

This time they all scrunched together in one vehicle. Gusta had stayed back at the pottery shop to wait for the police. Everyone had a seat belt, but it was still pretty tight. On the drive to the canyon, the adults were busy discussing the missing pottery and didn't notice the kids in the two rear seats conspiring to decode the clue they'd found. Marisa had her guidebook open and was scanning the pages for information on what she suspected was an ancient Indian language.

"Look," she said. "Don't these markings resemble the ancient writings of the Navajo?"

"Yes," Dani said. "I think you're right." Without warning, she grabbed Marisa's notebook and feverishly started jotting letters—she wrote them one way then scrambled them in a different direction.

"Look," Dani said. "If you play around with the letters, sort of like the ancient Navajo code writing, you can figure out what the clue says." She took the last letter from each word and moved it to the front. As she did this with each group of garbled letters, they began to form familiar words. Then she rewrote the words in reverse order and they began to make sense. Suddenly, '**LUESC HET OLDSH ANYONC HET**' turned into: THE CANYON HOLDS THE CLUES.

Grant was amazed at how quickly Dani had deciphered the code. Any doubts he had about girls disappeared in that moment. He was impressed—girl or not, this kid was incredibly intelligent.

Christina almost shouted out in excitement, but Marisa covered her mouth. When Nammie heard the muffled sound and glanced back in her rear view mirror, all she saw was Marisa's innocent smile and cheery wave.

Distracted in thought, Nammie was easy to throw off track. The kids put their fingers to their lips and Marisa snatched the notebook back from Dani. She scribbled: *Be quiet. We'll talk about this when we get a chance to be alone.* She passed the note around so each kid could read it.

Then they all shared a secret pinky handshake. They

knew without mentioning it, that if the adults found out about the evidence, they'd hand it over to the police and the kids wouldn't have a chance to solve the mystery.

They all grew quiet and focused their attentions outside the van windows, so they wouldn't be tempted to chat about the case.

All Christina could see was fog. What if it stayed like this all week and she never got to see the Grand Canyon?!

11 CANYON UNCOVERED

At the Visitor Center, Christina's disappointment mounted. According to Nammie, the Colorado River had eroded the canyon into a hole more than 200 miles long, 50 miles wide and a mile deep. Christina guessed she'd have to take her word for it, because today there was no hole, just a whole lot of fog. The canyon looked like it was filled to the brim with fluffy cotton. She couldn't see anything but the tops of a few trees and rocks pushing through the clouds.

"I can't believe it," Christina said, her voice trembled with the promise of tears. "Mimi . . . I'm *never* going to get a chance to see Grand Canyon."

"Just so you know," Marisa said in a quiet whisper so only Christina could hear. "Around here, the locals just say the canyon. When you say the *GRAND* Canyon, everyone

knows you're a tourist." Christina nodded with raised eyebrows as though entrusted with classified information.

Mimi embraced her granddaughter assuring her that the fog would lift, and they'd be able to see for miles and miles.

"Well," Dani mentioned, "one time the fog didn't lift for five days. Remember that, Mom?"

"That is true," Marisa admitted looking at Christina with a shrug. "But, let's keep our fingers crossed that this won't be one of those times."

"Let's go inside the Visitor's Center," Nammie suggested. "There are a bunch of neat exhibits and hopefully, when we come out, the canyon will be willing to show you her wonders." She gave Christina's arm a gentle squeeze.

Grant dragged his feet inside, looking as discouraged as his big sister.

Once inside the building, Christina's mood couldn't help but improve. There were displays of the different types of rocks found in the canyon, numerous photographs of the various plants and animals native to the area, and a really neat photo station where they sat in a kayak boat with a huge picture of the Colorado River roaring behind them. Grant whipped out his digital camera and took a

picture of Christina and her new friends. They looked like seasoned kayakers heading down the river on an expedition through the Grand Canyon. He was getting good at this trick photography thing.

Nammie stood next to a wall map of the Grand Canyon and its surrounding area.

"Have you ever heard of the Four Corners of the World?" Nammie asked them. She pointed just a bit north from the YOU ARE HERE box on the map and said, "Right here is the Four Corners Navajo Tribal Park. When you go there, you are in the only place in the United States where you can actually stand in one spot and be in four states—Utah, Arizona, New Mexico, and Colorado.

"Whoa," Grant said, impressed. "If I had four legs, I could stand in four states at one time!"

"The canyon is part of the Colorado Plateau," Nammie continued. "It was once at sea level. That's why the canyon is filled with fossils. Over time, it was shoved 5,000 to 13,000 feet upward to where it is now. It's amazing to see what erosion can do."

"Is erosion like an earthquake?" Grant asked.

"No," Dani interjected. "It's when the Colorado River cut into the Colorado Plateau. It took millions of years to wear it down one whole mile."

"Wow," Grant said. "Dinosaurs must have been here when all that was going on."

"That's right," Nammie said, " There's a place west of here where you can see a real three-toed dinosaur footprint."

Grant's mouth dropped open. *"Really?* Can we go? It would be so awesome to get a picture of a three-toed dinosaur footprint to bring back and show my class!" Grant was already thinking about what tricks he could do with his camera.

"It's summer, Grant. You don't even have a class right now," Christina said without enthusiasm. It wasn't that she wasn't interested in what Nammie had to say, but she was growing more and more impatient to see if the canyon had appeared outside yet. "Nammie, can we go outside?" she asked as politely as she could muster.

They walked outside and the canyon was still filled with fog. Christina kicked the dry dirt with her new pink boot, watching the dust settle on the suede. Suddenly, she felt warmth on her face. She lifted her eyes from her boots to the sky and saw the sun cutting through the clouds. As the sunbeams hit the canyon, it was as though a plug had been pulled from a bathtub, draining the fog from the canyon.

The canyon opened up, and the sun painted beautiful

layers of colors against endless sheets of sedimentary rock. Christina could hardly comprehend the beauty. There in front of her, as though it was created just for her, was a rainbow arching over the canyon. She could feel the sting of tears in her eyes. She felt Papa's comforting arm slip around her waist.

"Incredible," she heard him say, as he let out a sigh. "It's a miracle, isn't it?"

Christina tried, but she couldn't speak. The awesomeness of the experience was too difficult to put into words. It made her just want to be quiet and still. Grant must have felt the same way, because she didn't hear a sound coming from his direction. You know something has got to be pretty amazing to silence Grant, she thought.

"Wow, that sure is a narrow little creek down there," Grant finally said. "It's so...green." Grant's words split the surprising tranquility of the crowd that had gathered at the cliff edge.

"Uh, Grant," Dani said. "That's the Colorado River. It only looks like a creek because we are so high up."

"Whoa," Grant said. "You mean that skinny thing was responsible for all that erosion you talked about?"

"Yes," Nammie assured him. "It's hard to believe, but

just remember, it took millions and millions of years."

Suddenly, Christina felt something small drop on her foot and she tore her eyes from the panorama. She looked down to see a little girl bending down to pick up a white stone. Actually, a whole handful of stones had fallen from her pocket, but only one had hit Christina's boot. The little girl stood still, and her large brown eyes met Christina's. She looked nervous, like she just got caught doing something she shouldn't. Just then, a tall man with a dusty black cowboy hat and dark glasses grabbed her hand and yanked her down the path toward the canyon.

"Come on, Delaney," Christina heard him say in a gruff voice. "We don't have time to see the sights, we've got to get going."

As she was being pulled brusquely down the path, the little girl's eyes never left Christina's face. Why did she seem so desperate? Her dad must just be an impatient tourist trying to beat the crowds, *if* that was even her Dad. A chill suddenly ran down Christina's sweaty back.

12 Chasm Clue

Nammie planned to set Mimi up to do her research in the reference area of the Visitor Center, let the kids explore around the canyon, and head back to see if the police had uncovered anything about her missing pottery. She'd come back and pick up everyone later that afternoon.

Papa looked sheepish and finally spit out what he'd been thinking about all morning. "Nammie," he began. "Do you think Gusta would be interested in a little golf?"

Nammie cracked up laughing. "Oh, you better watch what you wish. He'll get you golfing ranch style out on a working cattle ranch where you'll ride horseback between holes and use cow pies for golf tees."

"No kidding?" Papa said. "That sounds like fun."

"Eww, gross!" Christina said. She turned her attention to Mimi. "Can we stay here and go exploring with Dani and

79

Marisa?" Christina pleaded. "You can pick us up when you're ready to leave."

"I'm not worried about them if you're not," Mimi said to Nammie.

"Oh, my," Nammie assured her. "These girls have grown up in the canyon. They know how to be safe and what not to do." She threw them a warning look. "I'm sure they'll behave."

"Speaking of what not to do," Papa said with a ghost white face. "Grant!" he yelled, "Get back here right now!"

Christina thought Grant had been right beside her, but now her eyes followed Papa's gaze out onto the edge of Mather Point, past the **DANGER** signs, to where Grant stood on the *wrong* side of the metal rail. There was nothing to stop him from falling right over the brink.

Grant was back to doing what he did best—spitting. Her brother, the master spitter, stood on the edge of the canyon making loud hocking noises and spewing slimy white froth into the canyon as if on a mission to fill the basin back up with foam. As the sound of Papa's voice hit his ears, Grant's body turned slowly and stiffly like a remote control robot. He climbed under the rail, dawdling and bracing himself for the inevitable lecture from Mimi on the importance of canyon safety.

"What in the world are you doing?" Mimi cried, grabbing Grant by the shoulders. "You could have been killed!"

Oh great, Christina thought. We were *this* close to being able to go out on our own, and Grant had to ruin everything.

Unbelievably, after a few minutes of ranting, Mimi allowed them to go with the girls while she went back to the Visitor Center. There was one stipulation. The kids had to give up one of the walkie-talkies, so Mimi could reach them whenever she needed.

As Papa ran to catch up with Mimi, he called over his shoulder, "Just remember...take nothing but pictures and leave nothing but footprints!"

"We know, we know," Grant and Christina recited in unison.

Only when they were out of earshot, did Christina say, "What were you thinking, Grant? You almost ruined our chance to explore without the adults."

"Not many people in this world can say they spit into the Grand Canyon," Grant said, a proud smile lighting up his face. "It was worth the risk...and the lecture," he said, then added, "I can't wait to go back home and tell all my friends."

"Yeah, if you live that long," Christina said.

"Let's go guys," Dani called from the trail.

Christina and Grant hurried to catch up. Marisa was even further down the trail, crouched down as though studying something. The other three ran up beside her and realized she had found something important, very important. It was another clue scratched on a dark metamorphic rock. It read: **URDENB FO EASTSB**. Dani scribbled the letters in her notebook and transposed them like the first clue. In no time flat, the words BEASTS OF BURDEN appeared.

"Wow! You are amazing with that stuff!" Grant said to Dani before he realized he was complimenting a girl.

"Beasts of burden, huh?" Marisa said, as she looked over at a stable where mules were tethered nearby.

Realizing what Marisa was thinking, Christina blurted, "That costs a lot of money. We can't go ride mules."

"Oh, but we can," Marisa said. "My friend's Dad owns the business. Sometimes he lets us ride for free if there are no-shows."

"What's a no-show?" Grant asked. "Sort of like those nasty biting no-see-em bugs?"

"No," Marisa said. "They're people who make reservations, and then don't show up for some reason."

"You guys," Christina argued, "Mimi will not be happy about this idea. We better call her on the walkie-talkie and ask permission."

"Oh, come on, Christina, what she doesn't know won't hurt her," Grant persuaded.

Yes, but what about the chance of *us* getting hurt, Christina thought.

13 COLLEGE-EDUCATED OR JUST PLAIN STUBBORN MULES

The kids filed into the line of tourists and listened to the trail guide explain an endless list of safety rules. Christina looked at the sweet-faced animals. She had never seen a mule wearing a saddle before.

"It's like they're pretending to be horses," she whispered to Grant.

The trail guide went on and on about how well trained the mules were—"college-educated" he called it. He said that though the mules were familiar with the rocky terrain of the canyon, the environment was unpredictable and there was always the risk of wild animals.

"You must always keep up your guard," warned the guide. "If the mule gets distracted or scared, he may lose his footing and fall from the trail. This could end in injury or even death for the mule and his rider."

"What?" Christina whispered loudly. *Death?*

Dani grabbed her arm. "Don't worry about it," she said. "He's just trying to scare you, so you stay careful." Oh, Mimi is really going to be upset about this one, Christina thought.

"The total weight on the mule's back cannot exceed 200 pounds," they heard the guide instructing. "Everyone must step up and be weighed before you mount your mule. Kids, feel free to pet the burro while you wait."

"Burro?" Grant asked.

"That's another word for a donkey," said Marisa. "Some people use that term for wild donkeys only."

"It kind of looks like a miniature mule, only shaggier," Grant said, looking at the burro thoughtfully.

"A mule is actually a cross between a horse and a donkey," said Marisa. "They are much better for things like this than horses are."

As the riders gathered in a line to be weighed, Marisa walked up to the guide and spoke in quiet whispers. After what seemed like hours, he finally smiled and pointed over to two mules near the end of the line.

"We get to go, but we have to ride two to a mule," said Marisa. "Which is fine, because none of us weigh over 100 pounds, so two will be less than 200 pounds, no problem."

"Okay," Christina agreed warily. Her gut was telling her not to go along with it, but her brain couldn't stop shouting inside her head about how much fun it would be. She got on the mule first, pulling herself up into the saddle, and then Marisa hopped on behind her.

"We get to ride Belle," Marisa said. "And you two are riding Bailey."

Grant and Dani mounted the mule in front of them. "Hi Bailey," Grant said, rubbing the mule's neck.

There were only four mules behind them in line. They were loaded down heavily with packs, but no passengers. The trail guide sauntered toward the kids and their mules, took one look at Bailey and ordered Grant and Dani to get off.

"Come over here and step up on the scale," he bellowed.

"But, we're just kids," Dani insisted. "We don't weigh much over 100 pounds put together."

"Well, something's weighing down my animal," he said. "Do as I say, or don't ride."

Christina watched as Dani stepped up on the scale, got weighed and then stepped down. Then Grant got on the scale. The scale leaned heavily to the right. Christina watched as Grant unzipped his cargo shorts pockets, one

by one, and emptied rock after rock onto the ground, until a shin-high pile accumulated beside him. Then he stepped back on the scale.

The trail guide cracked up laughing, tousled Grant's hair and sent him back to the mule minus his rock stash.

"Don't even say it," Grant warned Christina. "I just wanted to take them home for my rock collection."

Christina couldn't help herself. "Don't forget what Papa said about not taking anything," she warned.

Suddenly, a man riding a large mule butted in between Belle and the mule behind her.

"Move!" the man ordered.

Marisa gave Belle a little nudge with her foot so she would move forward. She had to stand sort of sideways in line to allow the other mule to fit behind her.

This made it easy for Christina to watch the man without seeming too obvious. She realized that right behind him in the saddle sat a little girl—the same little girl that had dropped the white stones at her feet earlier.

Christina said "hi" in a friendly tone and waved at the little girl, who couldn't have been more than six. She started to raise her hand in a wave when the man reached behind him and held down her hand.

"She doesn't talk," he said to Christina, squinting his

eyes hard like the rocks surrounding them. He gave her the creeps, but before she could mention anything to Marisa, the mules started on their way down the narrow and dusty Bright Angel Trail.

Christina was instantly distracted by the views and watching to make sure Belle stayed on course. Beyond the path, the canyon fell thousands of feet. Christina couldn't even see the bottom in some spots. Cactus with bright pink blooms rivaling the hue of Christina's hiking boots brightened dull corners of the canyon trail. Christina saw white-tailed squirrels—real live ones this time. She even saw a cat in the canyon. Marisa informed her that it was actually called a ringtail cat and was more like a raccoon than a domesticated kitty.

"Hey, Grant," Christina called out. "Watch out for the cactus. Remember all the cactus on our Alamo trip? You better keep your bottom up safe in that saddle," she teased.

"Very funny!" Grant shouted back to his sister.

Marisa giggled then said, "Look there," pointing at a spiky plant growing near the path. "That's the agave plant. It was food for the ancient canyon people. It flowers after 10 to 30 years and then it dies."

"That's a bummer. Just when you start to bloom, you die," Christina said. She was starting to get used to the

back and forth motion of the Belle's stride and actually began to relax and admire the wildlife and scenery. Her pleasure was interrupted by the disturbing buzz of the walkie-talkie. Uh, oh, she thought. It's Mimi.

"Christina?" she could hear Mimi's voice come over the line.

"Hi, Mimi," she said with as much innocence as she could muster.

"Where are you?" Mimi asked.

"Oh, we're just messing around on the canyon trails," she answered, knowing full well that not telling the full truth was just the same as lying.

"Okay, well, why don't you come on back for some lunch," Mimi suggested.

"Oh, Mimi..." Christina said, trying to think fast. "We've got water bottles, and trail mix, and beef jerky. Can't we just stay out here for a while?" Christina asked, almost sure she'd have to break down and tell her grandmother where they were, and that there was no way they'd be able to go back any time soon.

Marisa grabbed the walkie-talkie. "We've got lunch packed in our backpacks," she informed Mimi and handed the walkie-talkie back to Christina.

"Oh," Mimi said. "All right. Have fun and call me if

you need me."

Phew! "Okay, I will," Christina answered. She still had the button depressed when Belle started hopping and skittering from side to side, causing Christina to bump heads with Marisa.

"Ouch!" Christina yelped. "Whoa!"

"What's the matter?" they could hear Mimi asking. "Christina . . .?"

Christina did her best to sound normal and somehow convinced Mimi they were fine. Meanwhile all the mules were kicking and whinnying and carrying on, hopping and stepping fatally close to the cliff edge.

The children held on to each other and their saddles and tried to speak soothingly to the mules. The carrying on finally ceased and the mules didn't move. In fact, they refused to go forward. They refused to go back. They just stayed in one spot no matter how the kids tried to coax them.

Marisa tried speaking in sweet tones to Belle to encourage her to move, but she wouldn't budge, especially since Bailey, Grant and Dani's mule, was standing as still as a statue in front of him.

Christina heard the man behind them grow increasingly impatient. He yelled at his mule, "Move, you stinky

varmint," he said and kicked the animal in the sides with his hard boots. That guy has an anger management problem, Christina thought. Once again, her concern went out to the little girl. Christina started to wonder if they'd be stuck on this switchback trail for days. Would these stubborn mules move a muscle? Would they have to walk out of the canyon on foot? She blew out an exasperated sigh and as she rolled her eyes in frustration, she gazed at the canyon walls.

For the first time, she noticed the layers of rock that Mimi had spoken about. She could see for forever in either direction. She remembered she had said that the top sheet of rock was really 4,000 feet wide and was the youngest rock at 250-550 million years old. Funny what a mind remembers when it's stuck nose-scrapingly close to the side of a cliff. To her, the sheets of rock looked like the layer cake her Mom had made for her on her last birthday.

"Stumble here and you can kiss yourself goodbye," she heard Grant saying to Dani. That little guy always had a way of making her laugh, even in the worst of situations.

Finally, the guide walked down the trail towards them, being careful to stay between the mules and the canyon wall.

"No need to be alarmed," he said. "At least not

anymore. There was a wild cougar up on the rocks. My lead mule flipped out, then stopped in his tracks and refused to move and the rest of the group played follow-the-leader," he said with a tired smile. "Finally, the cougar decided to venture higher up in the canyon, so I'm sure the mules will feel more comfortable getting back to the business of walking."

He turned around and headed back to the front. "You can still see the cougar way up in the rocks if you look off to your right," he said over his shoulder. He got back on the lead mule and started moving down the path with the rest of the mule train moving on behind him.

"Wild cougars?" Grant said. "No one told me about the risk of getting eaten alive."

"Wow, I've only ever seen cougars in the zoo," said Christina, spotting the sable-coated cat sitting high on the cliff. The big cat watched the passing mules with wide eyes, like a kid trying to decide on a flavor at the ice cream parlor.

Suddenly, the sky turned gray and Christina worried that rain clouds were gathering overhead. She timidly lifted her chin, looked up in the sky, and was shocked at what she saw. Above them flew the most enormous birds Christina had ever seen. Their wingspan must

have been at least nine feet across. They blocked the sun and cast foreboding shadows over the trail.

"Whoa!" she heard Dani say. "Those are California condors—the largest land birds in North America. After almost becoming extinct, they now make Arizona their home."

Christina could tell the condors were scavengers by the absence of feathers on their heads. "I learned on a field trip to the nature preserve that scavengers don't have feathers on their heads, so they can stick them inside dead stuff and not worry about getting YUCK stuck in their feathers," she reported.

"Eww, gross!" Marisa said, as the last of the birds passed over and the heat of the sun returned to the path.

Even though the sun was beating down on her back, Christina couldn't shake the chill in her bones.

14 SIX SLITHERING SNAKES

This ride was no derby race—it was slow going and Christina's bottom was starting to ache with the bumpiness of Belle's gait. She was wondering when and where the next clue would show up. She was ready for a different mode of transportation.

She looked to the right and immediately noticed writing on the canyon wall. At first, she thought it might be another clue, but this writing was clearly different. It wasn't written in white and they were more like pictures with some symbols, rather than actual letters.

"That's terrible," she remarked. "My grandmother calls that graffiti. I can't believe people actually scribble on the walls of the Grand Canyon."

"That's not graffiti," Marisa explained. "Those are markings from different Indian clans who traveled by here

95

long ago on their trek to gather salt from the mines."

"Oh," was all Christina could say, silenced by the thought of being on the same trail that people had traveled hundreds of years ago.

They moved out into a wider open area where a huge flat rock jutted out over the canyon.

"This is where we'll stop for lunch," the guide instructed. "Everyone please get off your mules and let them rest. You can spread out over the rock, eat your lunches, and enjoy the view."

Dani picked a spot off to the side, a little closer to the edge than Christina would have preferred. The sandwiches and apples that Nammie had packed tasted good and the cool water quenched their thirsty throats, parched from the sun and dusty trails.

Christina noticed the man that rode behind them didn't join the group to eat lunch, but rather hung back with those last few pack mules. He circled the mules again and again, tightening the ties on their packs each time. She looked around for the little girl, but didn't see her.

"Where do you think that guy is taking those packs?" Christina asked.

"Oh, he's probably taking them to the Supai Village down in the canyon gorge," said Marisa. "It's the home of

the Havasupai Indians," Marisa said. "He's probably bringing special supplies down there or maybe trying to sell them trinkets to sell to tourists."

Suddenly Dani came running toward them white-faced with worry.

"Grant is in trouble!" she cried. "Come quickly."

Christina popped up and followed Dani out to the cliff edge, where Grant no doubt, had been spitting again. But this time he had company—bad company. Six snakes were slithering around his feet, heads held high, making sounds like shaking baby rattles.

Christina froze. This was serious. Those were rattlesnakes, one of the two venomous snakes found in this region. *Venom kills.*

"Grant, stay very still," Marisa instructed. But before the kids could run to find help, the little girl that had been riding behind them stepped right up to Grant and laid a burlap sack on the ground beside the snakes. One by one they slinked into the bag as though it was their home. The little girl, without a word, picked up the bag, tied a piece of thin leather around it and walked back to the man by the mules.

The kids stood in silent amazement as she walked up to the creepy man and held the bag up for him to take. They

couldn't see her expression, only the back of her head, but they could see the look on the creepy man's face. He looked like he was going to slap her. Instead, he snatched the snake bag from her hands and set it inside one of the packs on his mule. He glanced over at Grant, put on his dark glasses and roughly put the little girl on the saddle and mounted the mule behind her.

Christina grabbed and hugged her brother so hard that he lost his balance and fell bottom-first into a prickly cactus.

"YEOW!" he screamed. Christina pulled him up as quickly as possible, but not fast enough to keep a bunch of prickly spikes from embedding themselves in his behind.

"What the cactus just happened to me?" Grant cried. "I thought I was a goner!" He started pulling the spikes from his bottom.

Christina helped him pull out the prickles, apologizing nonstop and wondering out loud, "Is that girl a witch, or what?"

"Whoa," Dani said. "That was amazing."

"We've heard of children gathering snakes for the spiritual Hopi Snake Dance," Marisa explained, "but I've never actually seen a child handle snakes with such ease. They say that it takes about two weeks to gather enough

snakes for the ceremony and in the meantime, the children watch over the snakes. Miraculously, no harm usually comes to the children, but I would never try it."

Suddenly, the kids realized the mule train was moving out. They all hurried back on shaky legs to mount Bailey and Belle. Marisa moved Belle as far away from the man behind them as possible.

Just before the guide led the mule train onward, Grant caught a glimpse of another clue written on the rocks. He jumped off Bailey lickety-split. Carrying his trusty magnifying glass and Dani's notepad, Grant quickly jotted down the letters and hopped back on Bailey with time to spare. He handed the notepad back to Dani, grabbed the reins, and gave his mule a gentle nudge just in time to get in step with the moving mules.

Dani worked feverishly at decoding the clue, and she filled the other children in when they gathered near the old salt mines. She held up the paper, just so Marisa and Christina could see it, keeping it out of view of the man behind them. On the top of her paper were the scrambled letters: **ESERVATIONR IDER AFTR**. On the bottom, her decoded words read: RAFT RIDE RESERVATION.

"Does that mean what I think it means?" Christina asked warily.

Marisa nodded her head. "Yep. Looks like we are heading for the Colorado River." They jumped off their mules and followed the travelers around to see white crystals hanging from the side of the cliffs.

"What is that stuff?" asked Grant.

"It's salt," Marisa informed him. "This is where the Hopi came to mine salt. At that very moment, Christina's eyes looked upward to the sight of a red feather hanging from the salt crystal by a fine string. Her fingers suddenly constricted, pressing hard into her plastic water bottle causing a stream of cold liquid to splash right in Grant's face!

"Oops!" Christina apologized, but couldn't help giggling at the sight of Grant sputtering.

"Hey!" Grant snapped. "What are you trying to do—get me back for that soda disaster? I told you it was an accident."

"No...I...what's that?" she asked Marisa, pointing at the feather.

"That feather?" Marisa asked. Christina slowly nodded.

"That's just a *paho*, a feather offering for the salt mine," Marisa said. "Some Hopi Indians still believe in the old

tradition of offering up gifts to the spirits so that natural resources will remain plentiful."

Another red feather, thought Christina. Gift or no gift, the kachina stories and the red feathers were starting to get to her. Something told her they'd need all the help they could get to figure out this mystery.

15 LIGHT BULB MOMENT

They already knew the next step, when they got to the end of the mule ride. According to the clue, they were to jump on a raft, but to where? They stood at the stables rubbing their bottoms, especially Grant who had a few prickles still stuck somewhere in his shorts. Before leaving the stable, the kids said farewell to Bailey and Belle and gave them each a carrot as a token of appreciation for all their hard work.

"Why don't we have a snack too?" suggested Marisa, as she rummaged through her backpack for some trail mix and water bottles. "We can take a moment to come up with a plan."

Christina noticed the man from the mule ride was unloading his packs from the mules' backs. The little girl stood close by, fingering the white stones in her pocket.

Christina started to really take notice of what the man was up to—the way he handled each package so delicately, one by one, stacking them in wooden crates and shoving paper around the sides. He placed one box in a Jeep and then the other. He directed the little girl to get in the Jeep. She appeared to hesitate for just a moment, shot a desperate look Christina's way, and then seemed to change her mind and jumped in the front passenger seat—without fastening a seatbelt, Christina noticed. What kind of dad would let his daughter ride in the front seat of a vehicle these days without a seatbelt—unless, of course, he wasn't her dad. Christina couldn't shake the notion that the girl was in some kind of trouble.

Suddenly, a light bulb popped on in Christina's brain. Christina wondered if anyone noticed the flash. If those boxes contained what Christina predicted, that Jeep was headed to the river, to the rafts more precisely, and the kids had to get there as soon as they could!

"That man has your Mom's pottery," Christina said calm and confident. "I'm sure of it."

"What are you talking about?" Marisa asked.

"Look at him," she said. "Do you see the way he's handling those packs? He's got something very fragile in there."

"Are you kidding me?" Grant yelled too loudly. The man stopped what he was doing and looked across the way at the children.

"Shhh," Christina warned, attempting to act normal. "No, I'm not kidding you. I think that guy is the one who stole the pottery, and he's taking it somewhere down in the canyon."

"Why would he do that?" Grant asked.

"Well, Mimi mentioned the competition between some of the Indian tribes," Christina reminded them. "And Gusta said something about that black market. I don't know for sure why, but I'd bet my life he's got the pottery."

"River raft," said Dani. "Reservation—that's got to be the Havasupai Indian reservation. It's the only thing that makes sense."

"I just know that man is up to no good," Christina said. "And I think that little girl needs our help."

The buzz of the walkie-talkie startled the children and Christina dropped it into the dust like hot coals from a fire.

"Christina? Christina?" they heard Mimi call.

The kids looked at each other, silent fear mounting between them.

"You have to talk to her or she'll go crazy with worry," Grant said.

"Well, I'm starting to think she may need to start worrying," Christina said, pushing the walkie-talkie button.

"Mimi?" she said into the microphone.

"Christina, where are you?   What are you doing?" Mimi's voice blasted over the speaker.

"Mimi, I have something to tell you, and I don't think you'll be very happy," Christina said. "But, Mimi, I don't have a lot of time right now to explain. All I can tell you is that we are headed for the bottom of the canyon, and I think we need your help."

"Ahhhhhhhhhhhh!" is all Christina could hear when she let go of the button. Mimi finally calmed herself a bit enough to wail, "Christi-i-i-i-i-na!"

Christina held down the button and screamed into the device. "I know you're upset. I don't even know if you can hear me, but if you can, please come meet us at the Supai Village at the bottom of the canyon. We're going to go find some rafts, and we'll meet you there."

"Christina," Mimi said, just one decibel calmer. "Rafts? You can't go rafting down the Colorado River without me..." As an afterthought, she added, "Wear your life vests and be careful."

Marisa talked the mule trail guide into dropping them at the nearest raft launch on the banks of the

Colorado River.

"This is the place," Christina shouted, pointing at the rusty black Jeep parked diagonally beside the raft racks. The kids pooled their money together to rent a small raft, life jackets, and four paddles.

They weren't surprised when they found another clue on a rock near the raft launch. They didn't even have to write it down. By now they could all figure it out in their heads. The rock read: **TEALERS OTTERYP.**

They all yelled out in unison, "POTTERY STEALER!"

"I told you guys," Christina squealed. "He's a crook. I don't know what the deal is with that little girl, except that she's been scratching the clues on rocks with those little white stones. Bottom line, that guy is a criminal and needs to be stopped!"

They pulled on their life jackets and jumped into the raft and used the paddles to get the raft into the rush of the current.

"Hey," they heard a man's voice calling after them from the riverbank. "You can't take the raft out by yourself. Those are treacherous waters. You need a guide..." the rush of the water drowned out the rest of his words.

"Uh, oh," Grant said. "I knew we were forgetting something."

Before they knew it, they were traveling at lightning speed down the Colorado River and there wasn't anything *little* about it.

"I don't even have to ask," Grant said. "This is definitely *not* the Little Colorado River—it's the *BIG DADDY* Colorado River!"

The current pulled them down the river strongly and swiftly without any effort. Christina had expected to use the paddles to catch up to the other raft, but they were already picking up speed. Marisa, the most experienced rafter of them all, used her paddle to steer the raft through the protruding rocks. Suddenly, Christina heard rumbling sounds like someone had turned the jacuzzi jets on and turned the river into a bubbling hot tub—well, bubbling *cold* tub. What at first appeared to be an easy ramble down a babbling brook was fast turning into the runaway ride of their lives!

Come on . . . hurry!

16 RUNAWAY RAFT

"Uh, oh!" Grant said, as they came around a slight bend in the river. Just a few hundred feet ahead they saw the swift but smooth water churn and bubble into frothy foam. "What's up ahead?"

"White water!" Dani exclaimed. "Hold on to the sides. We're in for a wild ride."

They all held onto the sides of the raft, but Christina wasn't prepared for the bucking bronco rodeo raft ride. The raft buckled and bounced so hard that before she knew it, she was out of the raft and into the icy water, caught in the rush of the raging river. The swift current pulled her under; filling her nose and mouth with water and making her sputter, spit, and gasp for air.

"Christi-i-i-n-a!" she heard Grant shout with fear.

Then the rest was blocked out by the sound of the churning water.

Uh, oh, she thought. This was trouble. The water was C-O-O-O-L-D. *FREEZING* cold, in fact, and Christina winced in pain as her bottom bounced on the sharp rocks. She wondered if this is what it meant to hit rock bottom.

She looked back and screamed for help from her now frantically paddling brother and friends, but they were just too far behind. Finally, she came to an area where the waves weren't as rough and though she knew her Mimi would go bonkers if she saw her, she had to do something to save her bruising bottom.

She unbuckled her life vest, pulled it from her back, and slipped her legs through the armholes making a cradle to sit in—a sling to protect her backside from hitting the rocks. She found that if she put her feet first, she moved down the river more easily. She couldn't believe she was traveling down the Colorado River with nothing but a life vest. The trick was to get back on the raft with her brother and friends. She attempted to grab at anything she could find to stop herself, rocks, tree branches, but nothing could slow the swift current.

Before she could gather her wits, Christina got tossed around again in the river's white water rapids. She

swallowed large gulps of river water and struggled for air.

Then, without notice, she felt herself being yanked up by her shirt collar and pulled against the side of some kind of boat. She opened her eyes to see a bright yellow kayak, like the one they had gotten their picture taken in back at the Visitor Center. A man in a matching yellow helmet sat waist deep in the kayak, balancing his boat, while holding her by the collar like a newborn puppy.

"Hey there, girl," he said with concern. "You look like you could use some help."

"Yes sir," was all she could say in a small sputtering voice.

He held onto her for just a few moments until Grant and the girls caught up with them in the raft.

"Christina!" Grant cried. She could see tears in his eyes. "Are you all right?" They drove each other crazy like any siblings do, but in that moment, there was no one else she would rather have seen than Grant. She knew she could count on him.

"Yes," she said. "Just get me in the raft."

The man held on to the side of the raft as they floated tandem down the river for just a bit while Grant and Dani pulled a wet and shaky Christina back into the raft. Once Christina was safe back in the raft, the nice man let go of

the raft and glided behind them on the river.

"You kids be careful, you hear?" he called out to them, performing quick flips to show off his expert kayaking skills, waving his paddle and grinning in a wide friendly smile.

"Oh my gosh!" Dani said.

The kids all looked at her in wonder. "What is it?" asked Grant.

"Didn't you see?" Dani asked. The other kids looked at her in a collective question.

"That man," Dani said. "He only had one arm!"

The kids' mouths dropped open, and their heads spun around to where the man had been showing off his tricks.

When they looked back, the man was gone—he had vanished!

"Do you think that was the ghost of the one-armed John Wesley Powell?" Grant asked with wide eyes.

"I don't know who it was," Christina said, "I'm just glad he came to my rescue." She couldn't tell if the goosebumps on her body were from the cold river water or from the possibility that she had met a real live (or was it real *dead*) ghost!

Before Christina could think too much about helpful ghosts, she caught a glimpse of the man and the little girl

up ahead. Their raft had evidently gotten lodged on some rocks, and he was standing up rocking the raft in an attempt to break free.

Christina felt brave and ready to confront the man.

"What a creep," she heard Marisa say under her breath as she steered the raft with her paddle. She sounded ready for battle herself. "I can't believe someone would steal all my Mom's hard work."

"Greed makes people do horrible things," Christina said. She had learned that early in life from being involved in other mystery adventures.

"Too bad he doesn't believe in working hard to earn his own money," Dani said. "He'd rather take it from someone else. How can he live with himself?"

"Well, he's not going to, because we're going to make sure he doesn't get away with it," Grant assured her.

They synchronized their paddling and moved in a speed that probably rivaled the college crew teams Christina had seen on television. The kids amazed themselves at how quickly they caught up with the other raft. But when they did, there was only one problem.

"Now, what do we do?" Christina asked.

17 HELP FROM UP HIGH

Before the kids could make a move, the man, realizing he had been caught red-handed, surprised them all by grabbing the little girl and jumping into the chilly rushing river water. Christina was shocked! Neither the man nor the little girl wore life vests, and Christina feared for the little girl's life. At least he held her in front of him, sort of holding her on his lap, shielding her from the rocks. They floated swiftly down the river feet-first. This guy knew what he was doing, thought Christina.

The kids grabbed hold of the abandoned raft and Christina instructed Marisa and Dani to jump on board and check to make sure the raft indeed stowed Nammie's precious cargo. Sure enough, when Dani ripped open one of the bags, she pulled out one of

Nammie's prized pots. Dani squealed with delight, "We found them! We found them!"

"Awesome!" Christina shouted. "Now, you guys stay here and guard the pottery. Grant and I will go save that little girl."

"We will?" Grant asked in a small voice.

"You can't fight that guy by yourself," Marisa called after their raft that was already picking up speed. "You don't know how to steer, do you?"

"We don't have a choice," Christina shouted. "We can't let that little girl drown!"

"Where are Mimi and Papa when we need them?" Grant said, his shaking hands causing the paddle to wiggle in the water.

Just when the question left his lips, a sound of a thousand dragonflies descended through the canyon, whirling wings drowning out the rushing water. Christina looked up halfway expecting an invasion of giant bugs to whisk her away to another planet, only to see a much beloved red-baseball-cap-wearing Mimi hovering above them in a helicopter.

Through the bubbled window of the chopper Christina could see Mimi's hands waving and her mouth moving as though she were on a fast-forward video. She couldn't tell

We found the pots!

if her grandmother was yelling at her and Grant or cheering them on!

Despite the strong current, Grant and Christina were able to maneuver their raft over to the riverbank near the small patch of smooth rock where the helicopter had landed.

Mimi came running toward them, shouting with her arms flailing in the air.

"Mimi!" Christina shouted. "We need to go save the little girl!"

"What little girl?" Mimi screeched in horror. "Where are Marisa and Dani?"

"They are okay, they're up the river with the pottery," Christina said, as Marisa and Dani's raft came into view floating down the river. "But we need to use the helicopter to save a little girl from drowning," Christina insisted.

Marisa and Dani brought the raft full of pottery up to the river bank and Nammie jumped out of the helicopter to greet them.

"My girls!" she said. "You're safe."

"Yeah, Mom," Dani said. "We've got your pottery."

"That's wonderful, honey," Nammie said, hugging her youngest daughter. "But more importantly, you are okay."

They had to move quickly. Nammie decided to stay with

her girls and the pottery, while Grant and Christina ran toward the helicopter with their grandmother.

"We'll meet you down at the Supai Village," Marisa called after Christina, who was explaining as much as she could to Mimi over the whirling noise of the helicopter blades.

"You need to fly over the river, so we can look for the little girl," Christina said to the pilot, as he lifted the helicopter straight up into the sky like an elevator.

"No problem," the pilot said, raising his sunglasses. It was Gusta!

"Wow!" Grant gushed, as the vastness of the canyon came into view from 1,000 feet in the sky. "This is awesome. I've never been in a helicopter before. It's like being a bumble bee, without the honey."

"What's that smell?" Christina asked, turning up her nose.

"Uh, that would be me," Papa said from the backseat, sheepishly raising his hand and pointing to the cow poop on his boots.

"Eww, gross!" cried both children.

18 Cave Confession

The helicopter followed the river's path, as its passengers scanned the terrain for two floating castaways.

"I see something over there!" cried Christina. She pointed to a wet muddy patch with footprints leading away from the river.

Gusta landed the aircraft. They all jumped out and began scouring the area for signs of where the man may have taken the little girl.

"It's going to be tough to find them," Gusta warned. "There are a lot of caves down here in these canyons. A person could hide out here for years."

"Sort of like those terrorists in the Middle East?" Grant asked.

"Yep," Gusta said. "Sort of like that."

The group split up and canvassed the area inch by inch.

Finally, just off to the west a bit, Christina found a rock with one last clue scribbled in white letters. It read: **EM ELPH**.

Grant ran up beside her, and they both instantly deciphered the clue and blurted out, "HELP ME!" in harmony.

"They must be inside that cave," Christina shouted to the adults.

As Grant and Christina started running into the cave, Mimi grabbed them both by the arms.

"Just one minute, my little detectives," she said. "You are officially off-duty. Let Papa and Gusta handle the rest."

Papa rummaged through Christina's wet backpack to find the flashlight and soppy bandanna. He turned the switch on and shook the flashlight. It didn't work.

"Wet batteries," Papa said. "Good thing, we're prepared." He pulled the dry batteries from the plastic bag. As Papa and Gusta ventured into the cave, Mimi ran back to the helicopter and radioed the police for help.

Minutes seemed like hours, until finally Gusta and Papa emerged from the cave pushing the man in front of them, his hands bound by Christina's pink bandanna. The little girl clung to Papa's back like a baby gorilla, her dirt-smeared face lax with relief.

Just then, another helicopter with the word POLICE painted on the side descended from the sky. The officers jumped from the aircraft and apprehended the criminal from Gusta's grasp, just as Nammie and the girls pulled their raft alongside the other raft on the riverbank.

"Do you know how much I could have gotten for that pottery?" the man couldn't resist blurting, inadvertently confessing his crime.

"Some things are worth more than money," Nammie said, as she squared her shoulders. "Things like integrity and character and tradition."

"You are a bad man," Christina accused the man. "Not only for stealing from innocent people, but for what you put that poor little girl through." At once, the little girl jumped down from Papa's back and ran into Christina's arms.

"You saved me," she said. "Thank you."

"You can speak," said Christina. "Why didn't you say anything to us? We could have helped you much sooner."

"He said he'd hurt me, if I did," she pointed at the filthy robber.

"Well, no one's going to harm you now," said the policeman taking the child's hand. He told them that according to their files, the little girl had been kidnapped the week before from a family further up the canyon.

"Evidently, he intended to use her too as part of his elaborate scheme to con the unsuspecting Havasupai Indians into taking him in," said the officer. "He could hide out under-cover down in the canyon while he made his connections to sell his authentic pottery in the black market—a huge underground ring to supply ruthless wealthy folks with artifacts for their private collections."

He pulled the criminal by the arm toward the open door of the chopper. "Just a lonely widower trying to care for his poor sweet daughter," he said in disgust.

"Guess we put an end to that!" Christina said.

19 TIME TO RELAX

After the police took off with the criminal and little girl in tow, Gusta, Nammie, and Papa loaded the pottery into the helicopter.

"Are you coming?" Nammie called to Mimi and the kids.

"Oh, I thought we'd meet you down the river at the Indian village," Mimi responded.

"The only way to get to the village from the river is to hike in, horseback ride, or helicopter in," Nammie informed her. "The river won't take you there."

"I'm going with you," Christina blurted, running toward the chopper. The rest of the crew followed.

"Boy, that was a major flaw in that robber's plan," said Grant.

As Gusta brought the helicopter down into a cove in the little Indian village, Christina was amazed at the

aquamarine waterfalls and flowered trees.

"This looks like paradise," Mimi said.

"Ah," Nammie said. "We've made it to the home of the 'People of the blue-green waters'. Now we can relax and enjoy."

"You know..." Grant said, still thinking of the events of the last few hours. "This is a record. We solved the mystery in less than 48 hours!"

Christina, Grant, Dani, and Marisa all joined hands in a congratulatory high-five.

"We make a great team," Marisa said to her new friends.

"Yeah," Papa agreed, glad to have the mystery work out of the way. "Now we can take the rest of our trip to just kick back and relax...and maybe play a bit more ranch-style golf," he said, conspiratorially elbowing Gusta.

"Eww, gross!" said all four kids.

"Cow poop golf," Grant added.

"Well, one thing's for sure," Mimi said. "We won't be going on any more excursions—except to enjoy the beautiful swimming hole here at the village."

"Why not?" Grant whined.

"Well, let's see..." Papa said. "We had planned to take you on a mule ride..."

We make a great team!

"Check," said Christina.

"A white-water rafting trip..." Papa said.

"Check," said Marisa.

"And a helicopter flight through the canyon..." Papa said.

"Check," said Dani.

"Looks like we've done it all," said Mimi with a content, yet weary smile.

"Now, it's time for a nap," Papa said, already eyeing the hammocks hanging under the shade trees by the swimming hole.

"We'll get some good food," Nammie said.

"We've already got some good friends," said Gusta.

"All in a beautiful ancient Indian village," Mimi said. "Who could ask for more?"

Christina glanced up just in time to catch a floating red feather in her hand. She lifted her face to the towering cliffs to see the vision of the Indian warrior saluting her from above.

"Not me," Christina said, sending her own salute up to the sun.

The End

THE GRAND CANYON

Places To Go & Things To Know!

Grand Canyon National Park, Grand Canyon, Arizona – one of America's most popular tourist sites with nearly four million visitors annually; South Rim is open 24 hours a day, 365 days a year, and North Rim is open mid-May to mid-October; Little Colorado River and Colorado River run through the canyon.

El Tovar Hotel, Grand Canyon, Arizona – the largest hotel in the area, built in 1905 by the Santa Fe Railroad Company to accommodate the additional tourists the train would bring.

Lowell Observatory, Flagstaff, Arizona – the lab, founded in 1894, was responsible for the discovery of the planet Pluto in 1930; has a 13-inch astrograph (Pluto Discovery Telescope) and the historic Clark telescope; Mars Hill is home to five telescopes (two of which are used for the public), and six telescopes used for scientific observation at the dark-sky site.

San Francisco Peaks and Coconino National Forest, northern Arizona – highest mountains in Arizona; the peaks, which rise to more than 12,000 feet, are surrounded by pine forests and grasslands; prominent feature of southern Colorado Plateau; Mt. Humphreys and Mt. Agassiz are the two highest peaks.

Flagstaff "The City of Seven Wonders," Arizona – founded in 1894, the largest city in Northern Arizona, one of the highest elevation cities in the United States (7,000 feet); the city is nestled at the base of the San Francisco Peaks and surrounded by one of the largest pine forests on earth.

Navajo National Monument, northern Arizona – preserved site of the three most-intact cliff dwellings of the ancestral Puebloan people; sits on the Shonto Plateau, overlooking the Tsegi Canyon system in the Navajo Nation in Northern Arizona

Petrified Forest National Park, northeast Arizona – features one of the world's largest and most colorful concentrations of petrified wood, nearly 94,000 acres; also features the Painted Desert, historic structures, archeological sites and fossil displays.

Sunset Crater Volcano National Monument, Arizona – Sunset Crater, a 1,000-foot high cinder cone, is the result of a volcanic eruption which took place about 900 years ago; it is the youngest volcano on the Colorado Plateau.

Walnut Canyon National Monument, Arizona – sacred grounds with ancient single-story structures, cliff dwellings, built by the Sinagua people under limestone overhangs

Wupatki National Monument, Arizona – pueblo built by the Wupatki people less than 800 years ago

ABOUT THE AUTHOR

Carole Marsh is an author and publisher who has written many works of fiction and non-fiction for young readers. She travels throughout the United States and around the world to research her books. In 1979 Carole Marsh was named Communicator of the Year for her corporate communications work with major national and international corporations.

Marsh is the founder and CEO of Gallopade International, established in 1979. Today, Gallopade International is widely recognized as a leading source of educational materials for every state and many countries. Marsh and Gallopade were recipients of the 2004 Teachers' Choice Award. Marsh has written more than 16 Carole Marsh Mysteries™. Years ago, her children, Michele and Michael, were the original characters in her mystery books. Today, they continue the Carole Marsh Books tradition by working at Gallopade. By adding grandchildren Grant and Christina as new mystery characters, she has continued the tradition for a third generation.

Ms. Marsh welcomes correspondence from her readers. You can e-mail her at carole@gallopade.com, visit the carolemarshmysteries.com website, or write to her in care of Gallopade International, P.O. Box 2779, Peachtree City, Georgia, 30269 USA.

GLOSSARY

chert: a compact type of rock made up mostly of crystal clear quartz

silicon: a crystal element found in rocks & minerals; makes up more than 25% of the earth's crust.

crossbedding: sandstone that has lines or marks going different ways

sandstone: a rock formed of sand cemented together by silica, calcium carbonate, iron oxide, and clay

plateau: a flat area higher than the land surrounding it; often split by deep canyons

shale: a rock form of clay

travertine: a form of limestone deposited by springs

erosion: the gradual wearing away of rock or land by the action of wind, water, glaciers, or waves

fossil: the remains (such as a skeleton) or the impression (like a footprint) of an animal or plant from an earlier geological age

metamorphic: rocks that are created by being mashed inside the earth

SCAVENGER HUNT!

Recipe for fun: Read the book, take the tour, find the items on this list and check them off! (Hint: Look high and low!!) *Teachers: you have permission to reproduce this form for your students.*

__1. metamorphic rock

__2. binoculars

__3. sopapillas

__4. agave plant

__5. magnifying glass

__6. walkie-talkies

__7. kayak

__8. kachina doll

__9. rattle snake

__10. red feather

WRITE YOUR OWN MYSTERY!

Make up a dramatic title!

You can pick four real kid characters!

Select a real place for the story's setting!

Try writing your first draft!

Edit your first draft!

Read your final draft aloud!

You can add art, photos or illustrations!

Share your book with others and send me a copy!

SIX SECRET WRITING TIPS FROM CAROLE MARSH!

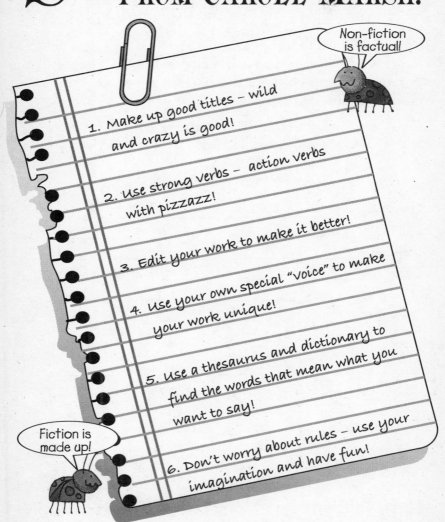

Non-fiction is factual!

1. Make up good titles – wild and crazy is good!

2. Use strong verbs – action verbs with pizzazz!

3. Edit your work to make it better!

4. Use your own special "voice" to make your work unique!

5. Use a thesaurus and dictionary to find the words that mean what you want to say!

Fiction is made up!

6. Don't worry about rules – use your imagination and have fun!

WOULD YOU ~~MYSTERIES~~ LIKE TO BE
A CHARACTER IN A CAROLE MARSH MYSTERY?

If you would like to star in a Carole Marsh Mystery, fill out the form below and write a 25-word paragraph about why you think you would make a good character! Once you're done, ask your mom or dad to send this page to:

> Carole Marsh Mysteries Fan Club
> Gallopade International
> P.O. Box 2779
> Peachtree City, GA 30269

My name is: _____

I am a: ____boy ____ girl   Age: _____

I live at: _____

City: _____ State:____ Zip code: _____

My e-mail address: _____

My phone number is: _____

_____
_____
_____
_____
_____
_____
_____
_____
_____
_____

Enjoy this exciting excerpt from

THE MYSTERY ON THE MIGHTY MISSISSIPPI

1 IN 1814 WE TOOK A LITTLE TRIP

Grant Yother stood in the middle of Jackson Square in the town of New Orleans in Louisiana and sang at the top of his lungs:

"In 1814, we took a little trip
Along with Colonel Jackson
Down the Mighty Mississip!
We took a little bacon and we took a little beans,
And we caught the bloody British in the town of
New Orleans!"

Then his grandfather, Papa, joined in:

"We fired our guns and the British kept
    a'comin';
There wasn't nigh as many as there was a
        while ago;
We fired once more and they began a'runnin'
On down the Mississippi to the Gulf of Mexico!"

Christina, Grant's older sister, and Mimi, their grandmother, hid their heads beneath the frilly umbrellas they had just bought in the Square.

"I've never seen those two before, have you, Christina?" Mimi asked, as they strolled away from the singers.

Christina giggled and rolled her eyes. "No! I certainly have not. I'm certain that those two are absolutely no relation to us, right Mimi?"

"Right!" Mimi agreed, steering Christina to an outdoor lemonade stand. They ordered two tall, icy lemonades and took them to an ice-cream parlor style table and chairs beneath an ancient oak tree all dressed up in thick beards of long, gray Spanish Moss.

"Isn't New Orleans just the most wonderful town?" Christina said. "I just love all the neat park squares, and the old trees, and the artists at work right out on the sidewalks."

Christina and her grandmother looked around. Sure enough in every direction all types of artists were scattered around the park "doing their thing."

Nearby a watercolor artist painted a beautiful scene of the park itself. Christina noticed how her pallette of colors glistened in the morning sun. Beside her, a photographer had a large camera set up on a tripod and was making a photo of a couple all dressed up fancy, old-timey costumes.

Down the walkway, a mime was acting out a humorous skit for a group of tourists. One of the children in the crowd giggled as the mime magically produced a red rose from behind her left ear!

"Is it always this festive in Jackson Square?" Christina asked Mimi. "It seems like one big party."

Mimi laughed. "Sometimes it does seem like New Orleans is one big party," she agreed. "Especially in the *Vieux Carré.*"

"What's that?" asked Christina. She knew it sounded like French, but she didn't know what the term meant.

"It means French Quarter," Mimi explained. "That's the area all around here where you see the parks, shops, restaurants, museums, tourist attractions, streetcars, and the riverfront."

"Hmm," Christina muttered thoughtfully. She had only been in New Orleans overnight and already she was captivated by the unique city. She and Grant and Mimi and Papa had driven down from their home in Peachtree City, Georgia and just arrived last night.

Mimi was a kids' mystery book writer and had come down here on a trip to research the Mississippi River. Papa was Mimi's official helper, travel agent, baggage carrier, and best restaurant-finder in the world, according to her grandmother. Christina and Grant were lucky that they often got to travel with them, like this time. School had just gotten out. The only deadline they had was to meet their friends Sam and Jake in one week in St. Louis, Missouri for some big Lewis and Clark celebration. Mimi was going to give a speech there.

While it might seem like Christina and Grant just tagged around after their grandmother, the truth was that Mimi had this problem—wherever she went, mystery seemed to follow! She always used her grandkids as real-live characters in her books. The locations and the history in the books were always real, too. But supposedly, the story was fiction—made up.

However, as Christina and Grant well knew, it didn't always turn out that way! While Mimi had her head in a book in some library, and Papa was off checking out historic sites, it often fell to the kids to solve whatever real-life mystery came up. That is, if one did—and it almost always did.

But this trip, Christina felt lucky. New Orleans was such a beautiful city. It still felt like spring here with a rainbow of flowers in bloom that smelled so good they made you smile. And the sky was so blue. And the grass lime green. And everyone seemed so happy, like life was a permanent vacation.

Perhaps, Christina thought, this would be one trip that could just be fun. Relaxing. No stress. No strange characters. No weird clues to decipher. No danger. No mystery.

Right?

VISIT THE CAROLE MARSH MYSTERIES WEBSITE

www.carolemarshmysteries.com

- *Check out what's coming up next! Are we coming to your area with our next book release? Maybe you can have your book signed by the author!*

- *Join the Carole Marsh Mysteries Fan Club!*

- *Apply for the chance to be a character in an upcoming Carole Marsh Mystery!*

- *Learn how to write your own mystery!*

THE CAROLE MARSH MYSTERIES SERIES